MY FRIEND TWIGS

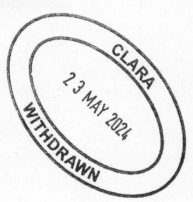

Also by Cliff McNish

Going Home

The Doomspell Trilogy
The Doomspell
The Scent of Magic
The Wizard's Promise

The Silver Sequence
The Silver Child
Silver City
Silver World

For Older Readers
The Hunting Ground
Savannah Grey
Breathe: a Ghost Story
Angel

My Friend Twigs

Cliff McNish

Illustrated by Abi Hartshorne

Orion
Children's Books

First published in Great Britain in 2015
by Orion Children's Books
An imprint of Hachette Children's Group
a division of Hodder and Stoughton Ltd
Orion House
5 Upper St Martin's Lane
London WC2H 9EA
An Hachette UK company

1 3 5 7 9 10 8 6 4 2

The paper and board used in this paperback are natural
recyclable products made from wood grown in sustainable
forests. The manufacturing processes conform to the
environmental regulations of the country of origin.

A catalogue record for this book is
available from the British Library.

ISBN 978 1 8425 5995 6

Typeset by Input Data Services Ltd, Bridgwater, Somerset

Printed in Great Britain by CPI Group (UK) Ltd, Croydon, CR0 4YY

For bird-lovers everywhere,
and anyone with an unusual friend.

Hope is the thing with feathers
That perches in the soul,
And sings the tune without the words,
And never stops at all . . .

Emily Dickinson

One

Is there an animal you love?

A dog, perhaps? Or a cat? Maybe something more unusual?

What about a bird?

Could you love a bird?

I have a bird I love.

He was my gran's, and she named him Twigsy-Twiglet. He's a cockatoo. But not an ordinary cockatoo. An especially rare type – a Moluccan. They're the biggest cockatoos in the whole world. With their salmon-coloured crest pointing straight up, they stand over two feet tall.

Amazing, eh?

Above is a sketch I did of him about a year ago. It's

one of my favourites because it's the last to include Gran.

Gran's on the left, just in case you thought that was me. She often dressed in that old cardigan. Dad's on the right. I'm in the middle, next to Twigs. My nose isn't quite that big. Twigs' beak is definitely that size, though. It's huge – like the rest of him.

My first clear memory of Twigs comes from when I was around four years old. I was over at Gran's house at the time, hiding from him under her dining table. All I knew was that this gigantic squawking white bird had just dive-bombed me from her couch.

Shooing Twigs away, Gran calmed me down and showed me a photo of a tropical island. It had rich golden sands, palm trees and a wide blue ocean that seemed to stretch to infinity.

'This is a photograph of Seram Island in the South Pacific,' Gran told me. 'It's almost the only place Moluccan cockatoos still exist in the wild now, Jess. They're incredibly rare.'

I glanced up, puzzled. 'Why, Gran?'

'Because everyone wants one, that's why,' she said. 'Moluccans are so gorgeous that they've been poached and hunted almost to extinction.'

I've still got that old photograph of Seram Island. It's crinkled and yellowed from the number of times I've held it. The colours have faded, too, and it's hard to see the details, but if you stare really closely you can still make out a few creamy-white patches fluttering under the palm trees.

Birds.

Moluccans.

A family of four.

'*National Geographic* magazine took this snapshot the same year Twigs was born,' Gran explained at the time. 'He's fifty years old this year.'

'Fifty?' I gawped, my four-year-old mind amazed that any bird could live so long.

'Oh, that's nothing,' Gran said. 'Moluccans are surprising in all sorts of ways. One in San Diego Zoo survived to be eighty-five years old. They live almost as long as we do. Do you know why?'

When I shook my head, she said, 'Because Moluccans are more like people than birds, Jess. They're really smart and sensitive. Twigs is always watching me, trying to figure out how I'm feeling. Even his heart beats at the same steady rate as a human heart.'

And that's when Gran did her trick, the one that made me remember that day forever. She placed Twigs (so heavy I gasped!) in my lap, took my hand and touched my fingertips to the downy white feathers on his chest.

The bird heart I felt there – *boom-boom* – scared me with how hard and fast it was beating. But when Gran turned my hand around, and placed it against

3

my skinny ribs, guess whose own heart was beating just as hard and fast?

That day was special for another, more horrible, reason: it was the day my mum died. She was killed on her bike in a crash on her way to work. It was awful, but I was so young that I don't remember much about her. It's Gran I remember. She moved house to be closer to Dad and me, and from then on I got to be with her almost every single day.

Which meant I got to see Twigsy-Twiglet almost every single day, too, of course. I grew up with him. I didn't have any brothers or sisters, but I had Twigs.

Gran taught me how to look after him. She explained about feeding and cleaning Moluccans – all those things you would do for any pet. But Twigs was soon much more than a pet to me. I spent so much time with him that he became my closest friend, and I know Gran felt the same way. How could she not? She'd taken care of Twigs for *forty-six years*. Imagine that!

'It's only me and Twigs now,' she used to joke after her husband, Granddad Billy, passed on. 'Only us two oldies left. A beautiful, cranky, noisy cockatoo – and dopey old me. All in all, I think I got the best part of the deal.'

Why am I telling you any of this?

Here's why.

Have you ever made a promise? I don't mean those silly promises to be good or behave yourself you make when you're a little kid.

I mean a *real* promise.

A *true* promise – one so important it can never be broken.

This story is about that kind of promise. I'm eleven now, and I made it a year ago. My gran had just died – and don't worry, it was a peaceful death in her own bed at the age of ninety-two – but it was still my wonderful gran who had faded away, and I hated it.

Not once during her last illness did Gran ask me to take care of Twigs after she was gone. She would never have done that. She was far too good a person to burden me with such a big responsibility. But I made a silent promise to her that I would.

I knew I couldn't possibly replace Gran in Twigs' life, of course. Gran and Twigs had such an amazing bond. They were lifelong companions. They were perfect together. I couldn't give Twigs anywhere near the same amount of attention as Gran, either. She could be with him almost all the time. I had to go to school.

But I swore to do my best. Twigs was used to a strong one-on-one bond with Gran. I'd make sure he had that with me, too. And whatever else I did, I'd take care of him and keep him safe. I'd never put him in danger.

*

But things happen, don't they? Things go wrong.

My dad restores ancient oil paintings for museums and, although he didn't want to leave our old house, he had to take up a job nearer the city to work on a big commission.

We ended up moving to a new home. It was miles from anyone I knew, miles from all my old friends. And it meant I had to start at a new school.

As I put on my brand-new purple uniform that first morning, and set off with Dad in the car, I had no idea what was about to happen.

I had no idea that for me and for Twigs everything – *everything* – was about to change.

Two

Ashcroft High School.

Eight o'clock, Monday morning. My first day. Eek!

Mrs Baldwin, my new form teacher, is the first person I meet. While Dad and I are filling in forms at the reception desk, she comes sweeping towards us, and my first sight of her scares me half to death. Short, with severely scraped-back greying hair, her chin is so pointy that she reminds me of the Wicked Witch of the West.

Striding up, she ignores Dad completely for a second and peers hard into my eyes. Then, I don't know what she sees there, but her faces softens completely, and she says in the most welcoming voice I've ever heard from a teacher, 'Fine. Jess, is it? Wonderful. Altogether good. Delighted to meet you. The Head has offered me the chance to teach you the embarrassingly little I know. What do you think of that idea?'

'Erm – OK,' is all I can think to reply.

Still nervous of her, I accidentally knock a sketch of Twigs I've been doodling at the reception desk onto the floor.

Mrs Baldwin bends down to pick it up. 'Intriguing,' she mutters. 'Who taught you to draw like this?'

'Er . . . no one,' I mumble.

'No one? Really?' Her bushy black eyebrows shoot up. 'You learned such accuracy of line and perspective entirely on your own? No one guided you?'

'Well, um . . . I did get books out of the library by artists, if that's what you mean, miss,' I say. 'I looked at, you know, how they drew things. Tried to copy them. Was that wrong?'

'Wrong?' Mrs Baldwin frowns, then flashes a wide-lipped smile at me. 'No, it's not wrong, Jess. In fact, I've been teaching art for countless decades here, but seeing your sketch makes me wonder if I should have spent rather more time in that library of yours myself.'

I realise she's complimenting me, but it's weird hearing something like that from a teacher I don't know.

'Are you ready to meet your fellow students?' she asks brightly, and I'm not, of course, but I nod, say goodbye to Dad, and follow her along two corridors to where the Year Six classes are.

Ashcroft High School is a private school, and the strangest thing about it is the small number of kids. Students from Reception through to Sixth Form are taught here, but the school only allows a maximum of ten students to a classroom, and with four students having recently left because their families moved away, the class I'm joining, 6B, is the smallest of all – there are only five students.

Mrs Baldwin opens the door and – *gulp!* – there they are, all staring at me from behind their desks.

Mrs Baldwin places her hands on my shoulders like a protective owl as she introduces me.

'Good morning, 6B. Let's give our new arrival, Jess Soper, a proper welcome, shall we?'

Murmurs come back from the class, and I manage a squeaky 'Hi!' as Mrs Baldwin lets me escape to an empty front-row desk.

There's a girl next to me. She's the only other girl in the class, and I'm getting a big friendly smile from her. At least, I think it's a friendly smile. It's hard to be sure, because her eyes are mostly hidden behind square, red-framed glasses and her frizzy hair covers half her face. She's chocolate-skinned, with a chin as delicate as a mouse's.

'Hello,' she says as I squirm into my chair. 'I'm Lucy Daniels. Do you like poetry?'

9

'Er . . . I suppose,' I mumble, because I've never really thought about it before.

'Good,' she says firmly. 'I'm a poet. I started very young. Of course, I wasn't very good at it then, and my poems were mainly about cuddly animals. Especially Fluffy.'

I raise my eyebrows. 'Fluffy?'

'My pet rabbit,' she explains. 'I wrote twenty poems when Fluffy was born. It was night-time. Very exciting. I wrote four hundred and twenty-seven poems about Fluffy before she died.'

'Impressive,' is all I can think to say.

She laughs. 'Stupid, more like, but I was only a little girl. Nowadays I mostly improvise poems. I'll make up one for you right now if you like. Pick a subject. Any subject will do.'

I wonder if she's joking, but when she smiles sweetly I see that she isn't.

'At the moment, I'm doing verses about pieces of furniture that no one uses any more, if that helps you choose,' she says.

'Furniture? Hmmm.' I'm not quite sure what she means, but I look around. 'How about a chair? Would that do?'

'What kind of chair?' Lucy asks. 'I like to be *really* challenged.'

Mrs Baldwin steps in. 'A *lonely* chair,' she says, and there are nods from the other students, as if they've been through this many times before. 'Make it a small, lonely chair with a comfy seat.'

'Lonely, small and comfy, huh?' Lucy grins, the tip of her small tongue poking out in concentration. A few second later she stands up.

'OK, I'm ready,' she announces, and says this:

'Little chair,
All lonesome and true,
Big bottom or small
You don't care,
So long as someone sits on you.
To stand is boring, to fight you need kung-fu,
So why not perch on this comfy seat
And enjoy the incredible view?'

My jaw drops open in admiration. It nearly kills me not to laugh, too, especially when what look like twin boys near Lucy pull faces, trying to make me.

'It's OK,' Lucy tells me. 'You *can* laugh. It's *meant* to be funny.'

'How did you make up the poem that fast?' I whisper to her, as Mrs Baldwin goes across the room to fetch some textbooks.

Lucy presses her glasses firmly onto the bridge of her nose. 'Oh, it's not hard,' she says airily. 'I've been making up poems every day since I was little. Last year my improvisations were all tragic, but I noticed people

11

didn't like those as much as the funny ones. That's why I mostly do comedy now.'

Mrs Baldwin quietens everyone down, and starts our lessons. She takes us through Geography and History for periods one and two, and during them I'm mostly able to tuck my head down and stay silent and unnoticed.

Sitting next to Lucy makes it easier, too. She's very intense about her poetry, but she's welcoming and friendly towards me right from the start. Being the newcomer still makes me feel edgy, though, especially when I find out that Mrs Baldwin has been the form teacher for everyone else in the class since Year Four.

At mid-morning break Lucy heads off somewhere, and I'm left standing in a corner of the playground feeling awkward. I shuffle my feet. I don't really want to be here, if I'm honest. I miss my old friends. Even more than that, I miss Twigs. I'd much rather be with him right now, but I can hardly bring a giant cockatoo into school with me, can I?

I'm nervously watching the kids from other Year Six groups when the twin boys from my class walk up to me.

'Hi,' one of them says.

He smiles, and so – in an eerily similar way – does the other boy.

Lucy has already told me about these two. Their

names are Hamish and Angus McTavish, and they're identical twin brothers. All morning I've been sneaking glances their way, fascinated by how similar they look. Both have the same light green eyes, snub noses and freckled cheeks. They even cut their black curly hair exactly the same way. It's all slightly creepy, but Lucy tells me they're the happiest and funniest boys she knows.

'Are you enjoying Lucy's poetry, then?' one of them asks.

'She, um, does know a lot about it,' I mumble.

'You can say that again,' the other boy agrees. 'She was too shy last year to say anything out loud, but this year Mrs Baldwin's been encouraging her. It means we get at least one new poem every day. I liked the one last week about a pencil stub.'

'The stub that was sad because it was too small to be sharpened any more,' his brother adds.

I smile, not quite sure what to make of them. 'Er . . . are you Angus?' I ask one.

'Hamish, actually.'

'Oh, sorry.'

'No problem,' he says. 'We dress the same way to make it harder for people to tell us apart. Means we can get away with stuff. Truth is, we've got nothing much in common, really.'

'That's right,' Angus chips in. 'Hamish is basically nuts. I'm not.'

13

Hamish grins and holds what looks like a shoebox towards me. 'Wanna take a look inside?' he says.

I try to peer over his hand. 'What's in there?'

'Only our hamster,' Angus says. 'His name's Hairy Jim. Mum bought him last week. A bargain. Only five pounds. He loves being stroked. Go on. He's really cute. He's just shy.'

Hamish slides the lid back.

It's a big mistake reaching into the box. Something black and slithering shoots up at me, coiling in my hair.

I shriek, knocking it to the ground.

It's a snake. A *mechanical* snake about five inches long. Both boys are laughing as they pick it up. Angus presses it carefully back inside its box.

'Sorry, Jess,' he says. 'Couldn't resist it. We call him Sid. No hard feelings, yeah? He's very real-looking, isn't he? Expensive, but worth every penny.'

Smiling at each other, the twins cart the box across the playground towards a Year Five girl sitting near the science block.

It takes me a few minutes to get over Sid the Snake, and overall it's a strange and long day. There's so much class stuff to catch up on. I've missed the first two months of the school year here, and the other students all seem to know a lot more than me about their subjects. Mrs Baldwin is reassuring, though, and stays behind in a separate office with me after the school day ends to help get me up to date.

By the time we're finished my head's spinning, and I'm anxious to get back to Twigs – he's not used to me being away for this long – but when I return to 6B to pick up my bag a boy is still sitting there.

Danny Davis.

He's the other boy in my class, and I've already decided I like him. I'm not sure why. Maybe it's because when I was standing at the front of the class this morning he waggled his fingers at me – a little welcome wave from his third-row desk.

Danny's got blue eyes and sandy hair, which he combs forward. He's tall, too – easily the tallest in our class – already looming over Mrs Baldwin. Right now, he's hunched over his desk, reading a book.

'Hi!' I say, trying not to sound too shy. 'What are you still doing here?'

'Nothing much,' he answers. 'Just looking at this.' He lifts the book up, and I see it's about dogs.

'Oh,' I say. 'Are you thinking about getting a pet, then?'

'Nah, just looking,' he tells me. 'Can't have a pet. Not a dog, anyway. Not allowed.'

He flips to a page showing a big dog sitting on a train. 'See this mongrel?' he says. 'Passengers call him Dmitri. He and some other stray dogs in Russia have managed to figure out how to use the train subway

15

in Moscow. They use it to get faster to areas where there's food.'

'Wow, that's amazing!' I say. 'How did they learn to do that?'

Danny shrugs. 'Oh, it's not that surprising. Dogs are incredible. They understand well over two hundred words, you know. They're really smart. There's a terrier in California who can juggle four balls between his paws.'

I glance up at Danny, not knowing quite what to say, but liking him. 'Um . . . are dogs your favourite animals, then?'

'Yeah.' He closes the book. 'I'd like to have one but . . . Mum won't let me. Too expensive to keep, she says.' He drops his eyes. 'Anyway, I have to go now. I'm late. See you later, yeah?' And, giving me a little smile, he slings his bag over his shoulder and heads off up the corridor.

As I walk back home – our new house isn't far from school – I spot Lucy. She lives only a few streets away from me, on Sidney Street.

I notice she's writing in a red notebook as she wanders along. It's one of what she calls her *poem pads*. She takes one everywhere she goes, jotting down 'rough ideas', she says, 'for perfecting later.'

I wave as she approaches, but she's so engrossed in

her poem pad that she doesn't see me until I'm right in front of her.

When I tell her about Danny and his dog book, she laughs.

'Danny's always had a bit of a thing about dogs,' she says, rolling her eyes. 'He spends all his time with strays when he's not at school. He's got a soft spot for one particular dog right now called Kim. She's lovely – an eight-month-old Rottweiler puppy. Danny's always borrowing her from the Fletcher family before and after school.'

'Borrowing?' I ask.

'The Fletchers breed Rottweilers to sell.' Lucy closes her poem pad. 'Their house is always totally over-run with them, so they don't mind Danny taking Kim for extra walks if he wants. They'd probably give her to him cheaply, but his mum says no. She's not a dog person. Danny's always trying to come up with fresh arguments to persuade her to take Kim, but she's dead set against it.' Lucy sighs. 'Actually, she's a complete *ogre* for not letting Danny have Kim, if you ask me. Anyone can see that the two of them are a perfect match for each other.'

Lucy pauses. Then she whisks open her poem pad to a fresh page and, with her tongue sticking out, scribbles a few lines. She finishes with a flourish. 'Would you like to hear what I've just written?'

'Yes,' I say.

Lucy raises the poem pad close to her lips:

'Danny without a dog,
Like a warrior unable to hunt,
Or a pig unable to grunt,
Or a tadpole unable to squiggle,
Or a worm unable to wiggle,
Or a clown unable to giggle . . .'

I smile, and Lucy glances searchingly at me. 'Any ideas of your own on that theme?'

'Oh!' I realise it's a test. She's asking me to *improvise*. I think hard. 'Um . . . like a mouse unable to nibble?'

Lucy snorts. 'Very good,' she says, and I feel like I've passed some sort of test.

'Like a giant without Jack to steal his gold,' she adds. 'Like a witch without her pointy hat. Like . . . a candle without a birthday cake.' She grins broadly, reaching out for my arm and squeezing it. 'It's been inspiring chatting to you, Jess. Thank you for reminding me that the spirit of poetry in class 6B is not entirely and completely dead.'

And with that she sets off again up the street, the tip of her pen already hard-pressed to her poem pad.

Three

Finally, I'm home – and Twigs, of course, is there to greet me. He's always crazily excited to see me when I first get back. My key is barely in the front door before he's huffing and puffing towards it.

'HERROOO, JESS! HERRRRROOOOOOOO, DARLING!' he calls out, just the way Gran used to.

Herroooo is Twigs' version of hello, of course. Except Twigs screeches it so loudly you jump. Well, Dad does. I'm used to it.

Twigs is a big talker. All Moluccans are. They're mimics – brilliant at copying things they hear. Twigs is super-good, though, even for a Moluccan. He repeats not just individual words but whole sentences. He invents his own sounds and words all the time, too.

MWAAAAA, *FFF* and *MOO-MEE-MOO* are his current favourites.

'DEARIE, DEARIE, *WAAAAAAAAAAAA!*'

Jump-hopping in his wobbly-bobbly way down from the couch, he dashes towards me. Twigs can't fly – Gran kept his flight feathers pruned to avoid accidents in the house – but he *can* glide short distances.

'GIVE UZ A SHMILE!' he croons, cocking his big wide head to the left, and I can't help grinning. Gran was always tickling Twigs under his chin and asking him for a smile.

'Hiya, Twigsy-Twiglet!' I call out, throwing my school bag down. 'How ya doing?'

'GRAAAAAAAA!' he squawks, loudly enough to blast the roof off. Then, after five more welcoming shrieks, he jumps up and down in front of me like a mad puppy. *'Paaaaa,'* he squawks. *'Paaaa aaaaaa.'*

He chokes a bit on the last *aaaa* because he's so thrilled I'm back. Now that Gran's gone, he thinks it's his job to keep watch over me. He's always relieved when I'm back safe and sound.

Standing up on his long grey claws, he lifts his creamy-white neck up as far as it will go.

'Th . . . th . . . th . . . th . . .'

He's after a kiss. Twigs is into kissing big-time. Gran made sure of that. He chases Dad for kisses all the time, too, but Dad always runs a mile if Twigs' massive beak gets anywhere close to him – which is

20

stupid, if you ask me. It's not as if Twigs hurts you. He only ever lightly touches his beak to your cheek.

After I bend down for a smooch, Twigs toddles around me. He's pretty fast for an oldie. '*MOO-MEE-MOO, MOO-MEE-MOO!*' he shrieks, and we do a few speedy loops around each other. '*MAGWA, MAGWA, pfffffffffffffffff!*'

'Hi, want a glass of orange?'

That last bit's from Dad, not Twigs. He's leaning against the kitchen door, his long arms folded. I notice that his brown eyes look a bit sunken and tired today.

'HERROOOOOOOOOOOO DADDY!' Twigs shrieks, greeting him with his usual wild excitement even though it's probably only a few minutes since he last saw him.

'Yeah, yeah,' Dad mutters under his breath.

You might be able to tell that Dad's isn't nearly so keen on Twigs as I am. 'Way too noisy,' he'd groan while Gran was alive, but after she died he took Twigs into our house without complaining. Until recently, that is. Recently, Dad's been complaining *a lot*!

I can't blame him, I suppose. Twigs *is* noisy. Incredibly noisy, sometimes. Other birds chirp, tweet and twitter. Twigs does all of that, but like all members of the large parrot family he also squawks, squonks, hoots and SCREECHES. On top of that he'll suddenly SCREAM his head off whenever he feels like it – which is often.

21

'GREEEEEEOOOOOOOOOOOOOOOOOO!' he blasts now, so happy to see everyone in the family together again that his peach-coloured crest (actually, its proper name is a *recumbent*) stands straight up.

Dad cringes at the noise. I never really understand why. Yes, I know Twigs is loud, but the only reason he's making such a racket is that he's happy. He's super-excited about life, that's all!

Anyway, Dad's the last one who should complain. He works in a separate room. By the time I'm home Twigs has been alone most of the day, so *of course* he's bursting to talk to me!

'GALA-GALA-GEENY!' he calls out, and I laugh. *Gala-gala-geeny* is a new phrase he invented only last week.

'Glad you're back,' Dad says, unable to hide a huge sigh of relief that I'm back.

'WOOO-HOOOOOO!' Twigs hoots, doing his owl impression, followed by a head-ripping 'EEEEEEEE!' that nearly breaks Dad's eardrum.

'Ouch,' I wince. 'Sorry. That was a noisy one. It just means he likes you, of course.'

'You could have fooled me.' Dad shakes his head, managing a rueful grin. 'What was your first day at school like?'

'Not bad,' I tell him. 'Mrs Baldwin taught us all about glaciers, limericks and the Romans.'

'As for me,' Dad says, after I've told him how school

22

went, 'thanks to Mr Twiglet here, I've been learning a lot about *gaaaaa, muuuueeeee* and *wawawa.*' He plumps a cushion on the sofa. 'I've watered him and cleaned out his cage for you, by the way. Oh, and I got another toy for him before he completely destroys the couch.'

Dad shows me a special bird mobile made from wood, rubber and long twisty bits of rope. It's either buy toys like this or Twigs shreds the furniture. Twigs loves wrecking things, especially when he's bored. I'll admit that's a problem, but if Dad just learned to *play* with him, it wouldn't be!

Gently head-butting my shin (he *loves* head-butting), Twigs stares up at me happily with his huge, bright blue eyes.

'OOOOOO-EEEEE,' he says. 'OOOO-EEEEE . . . OOO-EEEE . . . OOO-EEEE . . . OOO-EEEE . . . ooo-eeee . . .'

There. Hear that? What's Dad moaning about? Twigs is quietening down now that he's had a chance to say a proper hello. Soon he's up beside me on the couch, nestling against my leg.

'Gratitude, eh?' Dad mutters. 'Look at him now you're back – affectionate as a kitten!' He manages a frustrated laugh. 'I wish he'd save some of that lovey-dovey stuff for me.'

'Shut up!' Twigs squawks at him, and I chuckle. Twigs is saying *'Shut up'* a lot at the moment. Dad

23

generally bites his tongue about it because we both know he taught him that one.

'Swishy-sweee! Swishy-swoooo!'

Hopping onto his wooden climbing frame at the back of the living room, Twigs dashes up and down the knotted ropes. 'Jumpy up up!' he cries, repeating a mixed-up version of words Gran used to say to him. 'Jumpy downy down down . . . slidey slidey.'

'That bird's sheer enthusiasm for life is unnerving,' Dad says, brushing the edge of the couch. 'He's shedding powder again, by the way. Does that mean he's unhappy or something?'

I roll my eyes. Dad's just moaning. He knows only too well that Molluccans constantly shed a white powder. The powder comes from special downy feathers and is completely harmless, though I have to admit it gets everywhere. But it's not like Dad to mention it. He sounds really fed up with Twigs today. If I'm honest, he's been tetchy for weeks now. It doesn't help when – as Dad heads to the kitchen – Twigs marks out each of his footsteps with a squawked, '*Waa-waa-waa-waa.*'

Twigs is always making funny noises like that at Dad. He plays tricks on him, too. Hides his slippers. And his keys. And his gloves. He's only doing it to get Dad to chase him – Twigs likes the attention – but Dad rarely does. Even now, Dad can only sigh at all the *waa*s. He knows Twigs is just being cheeky but, unlike me, he doesn't find the joke funny.

24

'Shush,' I mutter to Twigs, but he isn't listening because he's tearing chunks out of the new toy Dad bought him.

Dad comes back in from the kitchen with an orange juice for me and a bacon sandwich for himself.

'BACON BUTTY!' Twigs screeches, running up to him and sniffing the sandwich. 'Bacon butty! Daddy likes a bacon butty! Wanna sandwich? Waaaa! Wanna sandwich? Waaaaaaaaa! Tasty. Scrunchy. Tasty. Scrunchy. WAAAAAAAAAAAAAAAAAAA!'

This goes on a while, because Twigs always gets incredibly excited by food.

Dad holds his breath while he waits for Twigs to quieten down again. 'Are you finished?' he asks when Twigs finally closes his beak.

'GIVE UZ A KISS!' Twigs screams at him.

'Not a chance,' Dad mutters.

Since Dad's in such an off mood, I grab Twigs and whisk him upstairs.

My bedroom is on the second floor of our new house. It overlooks the back garden, and I spend a lot of time up here whenever I'm home, to make sure Dad gets a proper break from Twigs.

Today – as usual – the first thing Twigs and I do is play a few run-around games. That way he can let off some energy.

Afterwards I phone some of my old friends. I haven't seen any of them since we moved here a few weeks ago, but we stay in touch. Dad's planning to take me back on a visit to see them, but it won't be for a couple of weeks yet.

Once I've caught up with their news, I sit back and do a few sketches. I spend most of my spare time drawing. I've always drawn a lot. These days I mostly sketch things in the house and stuff I can see from my new bedroom window. I used to sketch outside as well, but since Gran died Twigs needs me more so I usually come straight back home from school. Not that I mind giving Twigs the extra attention. He'd do the same for me.

When I'm tired, like now, I mostly just doodle-draw, making up stuff.

It's October, so the sky begins to darken early. For Twigs, that's a signal. The moment he sees the sun start to set he runs across my mattress and jams his big squishy face up against the window.

'Roooooo!' he croons, throwing his head excitedly from side to side. 'Roooooooooo! Roooooooooooo!'

The first time I saw Twigs gaze at a sunset like this was at Gran's house, and I couldn't figure out why he was so eager. It took me ages to realise that he likes to see the garden birds. Sunset is the best time for this because that's when all the birds return to the trees before they roost.

Our new garden is even better than Gran's for seeing birds. Two wide beech trees right outside my window are always full of sparrows and finches.

Mornings are like this, too, but then Twigs doesn't just watch the birds. He *joins in* with the dawn chorus – copying all the little cheeps and chirps. He's careful not to wake me up, though. He does it quietly, keeping his beak nearly shut. That's how thoughtful he is, you see. One way or another, he's always taking care of me.

Studying him now, hushed like this, so *still*, leaning against my shoulder, staring out at the other birds, is always when I notice how amazing Twigs is. I mean, he looks beautiful all the time, of course. There's no bird in our country to match his huge size or his lush, creamy-white feathers. But in the evening light there's a gloss to Twigs' plumage as well. It's a sort of peachy flush. The undersides of his wings are so richly orange that they look like they've been dipped in oils. I often try to capture those gorgeous tints when I draw him with my full set of coloured pencils, but I never can.

This evening – while Twigs is distracted by the twittering birds – I play a sneaky trick on him. I open the window a crack. It's something I've been doing for two weeks now, leaving the window open a bit more each day. Why? Because I'm trying to get Twigs used to the feel of the wind. It scares him.

How can a bird be scared of the wind? you're probably thinking, but that's because you don't know Twigs' past. His first owner, Harry Smith, never let him go outside.

'Isn't that terrible?' Gran said to me years ago, and I can still remember how angry she looked. 'Moluccans weren't a protected species in those days, Jess. Twigs was torn from his nest on Seram Island when he was only a chick. Then he made a whole month's journey in a dark box all on his own on a bumpy ship. Imagine that! It's incredible he survived at all. And as for Harry Smith . . .' Gran's lips narrowed. 'Well, that horrible man treated Twigs very badly. Kept him mostly in his cage. And never let him go outside into the garden.'

'Why not?' I asked.

'The stupid man was worried Twigs would fly off, that's why.' Gran shook her head. 'All he had to do was clip his wing feathers, but Harry Smith was too lazy to bother. By the time I rescued Twigs five years later, he was too scared to go outdoors. No matter how gently I carried him into the garden, he always ran straight back in.'

'But what about now, Gran?' I remember asking. 'Can't Twigs go out now? Does he still not feel safe enough?'

Gran sighed. 'Twigs is way too old to change now, Jess. He's just an elderly gent who likes his blanket and his chewy toys.' She grinned. 'Plus a noisy chat sometimes, of course, and a cosy bit of central heating. But he'll never set foot outside a house.'

Mm. Maybe Gran was right about that. But I sometimes wonder if she might have given up a bit too soon on coaxing Twigs to go outside. I'm trying to get him used to *feeling* the wind, at least.

Tonight, though, Twigs sees what I'm up to. Giving me a grumpy glance, he wiggles his tail feathers suspiciously and says, 'Bleeeeeeaaaaaaaaaaaaa . . .'

'It's OK,' I whisper. 'Go on. Why don't you have a peep outside? It's nice out there. See what you think.'

I shove the window open wide enough for Twigs to thrust his head out. It's the first time I've ever done that, and I hold my breath. Will he chance it?

Uh-uh. I've pushed him too far. Staring at me as if I've betrayed him, he scrambles away from the windowsill.

While I stroke his neck, a sparrow *chrrrrrrs* outside. In response, Twigs *chrrrrrs* back and stares miserably at me.

'Go on,' I whisper. 'There's only grass and birds out there. Nothing's going to hurt you. Say hello.'

And for a second I think Twigs might. He definitely edges towards the window as if he wants to. Then a gust of wind springs up. It's only light, but it's enough to send him squawking in panic back to me.

'It's OK, it's OK,' I say, clutching his shaking body. 'It's only a little sparrow saying hello.'

'*Mwwwaaa!*' he cries, trembling and tucking up against me for reassurance.

I shut the window and cuddle Twigs, holding him close the way he likes, until he feels safe again.

With him tight in my arms, I can't help thinking of my promise to Gran. I'm sure Twigs would love the garden. He just needs to get over his fear! If I can just get him to go outside, think how much better his life will be. He'll be able to do all sorts of new things, like play in the grass and make friends with the other birds!

And, if I'm honest, there's one more thing I'd like to do for Twigs.

I'd like him to *fly*. Every bird should be able to fly, shouldn't it? It seems so wrong that he's never had the chance.

Gran was always strict about that. She kept Twigs' flight feathers regularly clipped. 'Imagine what would happen if he flew off!' she told me. 'I can't risk that. What if he got lost? If he couldn't find his way back home he'd starve, Jess. He's always been hand-fed. He wouldn't have a clue how to find his own food. And do you think for a moment Twigs could defend himself? Of course not! He's been indoors his whole life. The first fox he met would gobble him up for lunch!'

Gran was right to be cautious about all those things. But does that mean Twigs should never have a chance to fly? I've got to keep him safe, of course, so I'd have to find a secure spot for him to spread his wings, but there must be places like that – enclosed, protected.

Those are my dream-wishes, anyway – the dream-things I'd like to do for Twigs.

But whatever happens, I won't break my promise. I'll keep Twigs with me, just like Gran did. I'll be company for him. I'll make sure I keep him safe. And no matter how hard things get, I'll never, ever let anything separate us.

Four

My second day at Ashcroft High is hard. I'm having to learn so much new stuff! Twigs makes up for it, though, by being so pleased to see me when I get back.

Scuttling past Dad, he lets out a piercing, 'HERRRROOOO, JESSIE DEAR!'

'Hi, Twigsy!' I say, bending down for a quick kiss.

'WHOOOO-WAAAAAA!' he shrieks.

'Ah! New word, eh?' I compliment him. 'I like it!'

'Yeah, delightful, isn't it?' Dad grunts, looking tired. 'I've been hearing it all day.'

Seeing that Dad seems to be in an irritable mood again, I take Twigs straight upstairs to get him out of the way. Nudging me to give him room on the bed, he nestles close, waggling his tail while I do my homework.

A bit later – *'Rooooooo!'* – a seagull flies overhead, and Twigs gets so excited that he entertains me with his bobbing dance, flinging his head wildly from side to side. All Moluccans love bobbing.

When he gets bored of that, he hangs upside down from the curtain rail for a while, then heads to his cage.

A cage? you're probably thinking. *He still has a cage?*

Well, yes, but only because all cockatoos need an enclosed space where they feel safe. Twigs' cage is a large round metal-wired one I inherited from Gran. I've taken the door off, and Twigs doesn't ever have to go in unless he wants to, but he still sometimes prefers relaxing and sleeping inside.

It's while he's resting on his perch, having a nap, that I hear voices I recognise.

I gaze out of my bedroom window to see Danny and the twins walking along the lane that runs just behind our back garden.

A dog is trotting beside them. A black dog with brown patches. It's big, but from the way it's springing along, tripping over outsized paws, I can tell it's young.

Ah, I think. *It must be Kim, the puppy Lucy talked about.*

For a second I'm nervous – should I go out to say hello to them? Maybe they'll be annoyed if I butt in. I chew my lip, undecided, but as their voices grow more distant I decide to brave it. Giving Twigs a quick kiss, I slip my shoes on and run downstairs.

'Dad, can I go and talk to a few kids from my class?' I ask. 'They're just outside.'

Dad agrees, on condition that I don't go further than the park near our house.

As I run to catch up with the boys, I can hear Danny saying to Kim, 'Hey, how long should we stay out? Until it's dark? OK, till it's dark! Were you lonely without me? Ha! 'Course you were!'

Kim's tail flicks around in high, relaxed swishes. Danny has her on a lead, but he doesn't need it. It's obvious how much she trusts him.

'Hi, Jess,' Hamish calls out when he sees me coming.

'Hey!' I say, hurrying across. 'I heard you from my house. I live just over there. Is this Kim?' I kneel beside them. 'Can I stroke her?'

Angus laughs. 'You can try.'

As soon as I do, Kim's tail shoots straight between her legs. She retreats, skulking behind Danny's knees.

'Don't take it personally,' Hamish says. 'Kim's like this at first with everyone she meets. She's a right scaredy-cat.'

'No, she's not,' Danny grunts.

'Yeah, she is,' Angus says, 'and you know it. She'd run from a kitten. Here, rub her belly, Jess. She likes that.'

He turns Kim over, and at first I hold back – I'm

34

not sure I want to get too close to those gleaming white teeth of hers. But as soon as I'm tickling her tummy Kim's tongue flops out like a sock, and she lifts her paws in surrender.

'There, you're friends now,' Hamish says. 'Jess, meet Kim, the softest dog in the world.'

'She's *not* soft,' Danny mutters, but he's smiling.

We head to the small park, and I rub Kim's flank, glancing sidelong at Danny. 'She's lovely,' I say. 'How did you meet her?'

'She was on a walk,' Danny says. 'I saw her being a bit dominated by the other Fletcher family dogs.'

'Kim comes from a litter of five,' Angus adds. 'The Fletchers are more than happy for Danny to do all their dog-walking for them.'

Hamish grins. 'Yeah. He's around their house so often they've bought him his own lead!'

Danny shrugs self-consciously at me. 'It's not like that, Jess. I just take her out. You know, give her a bit of extra attention sometimes. Stuff like that.'

'There's no chance they'd let you keep her?' I ask.

'Danny's mum doesn't like dogs,' Angus says.

'She *does* like dogs,' Danny mutters. 'She just . . . doesn't know it yet.'

When that gets a big laugh from the twins, Danny gives me a rueful look and plays with Kim's ears. 'It's true, Mum's dead set against a dog right now,' he grudgingly admits. 'But people change their minds, don't they? I just need to convince her. I've already told her how amazing dogs are at guarding a house.'

'And a dog is a loyal friend as well,' Hamish adds. 'That's two solid reasons.' He turns to me. 'We're going over to Danny's house right now to help him persuade his mum. Why don't you come with us, Jess? It'll be four against one.'

They wait while I check with Dad, and since the address is so close to our house he lets me go as long as I'm back before dark.

We drop Kim off at the Fletchers on the way, and Danny makes a big fuss over her before she goes in.

When we get to his house, Danny's mum greets us at the door. She's a tall woman, broad-shouldered with cropped black hair. Seeing the twins, her eyes narrow suspiciously, as if she's dealt with them before.

'Hello, Angus,' she says to Hamish. 'How's Sid the Snake? Still scaring mums up and down the country?'

'Well done! You got my name right this time!' Hamish says, his eyes lighting up happily at her mistake. 'I'm so sorry Sid fell out of his box the last time we were here, Mrs Davis. I dunno how that happened.'

'Hmmm.' Folding her arms, Danny's mum says hi to me. 'Have you come to persuade me that having a dog is the best thing in the world?' she asks with a grin. 'Because that's what Danny normally brings people home for.'

'Er, um, no,' I say. 'I'm just . . . er . . .'

Making a quick excuse to his mum, Danny leads me and the twins straight upstairs to his room before I completely mess things up.

Once we're settled, Angus says, 'What we need is a killer argument for keeping a dog. An argument she can't resist.'

When all three of them gaze at me, I gulp.

'Erm, I'm not sure if this helps,' I say finally, 'but I was reading that dogs can smell much better than us, so they're good at warning you if there's a fire.'

A huge smile spreads across Danny's face. 'Of course!' he cries. 'That's it! They *save your life*. Brilliant!'

'Yep,' Angus says. 'How about drawing it for us?'

I shrink back. 'Draw it?'

'Yeah. Go on. We've seen you sketching in class. Can you do a cartoon or something? Maybe if we can make Danny's mum laugh, she'll stop being so grumpy about dogs.'

'All right,' I say hesitantly. 'What kind of paper have you got?'

Danny finds a pencil and an A4 pad. It's not my usual sort of drawing, but after a few minutes I come up with a sketch of a dog running from a house on fire, dragging a woman who looks like Danny's mum in its jaws.

'Fantastic!' Angus says. 'Danny, your mum is going to love this. Go down and show her.'

Danny tramps downstairs with the sketch. A minute later we hear a bark of laughter. It sounds like a dog's bark, but I'm pretty sure it's his mum's voice.

'Didn't work, eh?' Hamish mutters when Danny returns. 'Never mind. I had an idea while you were down there. Your mum's a bit bossy, yeah?'

'Definitely,' Danny agrees.

'OK. So tell her that dogs are great because you can order them about. They don't mind. In fact, dogs love obeying commands. She can tell a dog what to do all day long.'

I end up sketching a dog standing on its hind legs at the kitchen sink doing the dishes, with Danny's mum beside it saying, *'And when you've finished all that, make me a pizza.'*

'You're good at this,' Angus says to me.

Danny takes the drawing downstairs. There's more laughter from his mum.

'She's a tough nut to crack, that's for sure,' Hamish admits when Danny comes back shaking his head again. 'But she's laughing. That's got to be a good sign.'

'It's stupid!' Danny sits heavily on his bed. 'I'll never persuade her. Too expensive. That's what she always says. *Too expensive.* Especially a big dog like Kim.'

'Don't lose heart,' Angus says, patting him on the back. 'We've made real progress. Anyway, we're off now. Mum'll kill us if we're not back by five. See you later.'

And without another word the twins head, side by side, down the staircase and out the door.

Danny walks me home. He doesn't talk much on the way. I realise he's upset about Kim.

'If you come up with any fresh killer arguments, let me know, yeah?' he says as we part company. 'That one about fires was great. There must be some way to get through to Mum.'

'OK,' I tell him, smiling. 'See you at school tomorrow.'

Five

'HERRRROOOOOOO, JESSIE!'

Twigs throws himself at me as soon as I get home. He's so pleased to see me that he head-butts my knees five times.

'Rooooo. Rooooooo. Roooooo!'

There's no sign of Dad. It's only when I go looking, and find him slumped over the chair in his study, that I realise something's badly wrong.

'Dad?'

'Oh, you're back!' He quickly straightens up, running his fingers through his hair.

'What's wrong?' I ask, following him to the living room.

'Nothing's wrong . . . nothing at all, Jess.'

'No,' I say, pulling Twigs onto my lap. 'Tell me. What's going on?'

Dad hesitates, then slowly makes his way across the room to sit next to me on the sofa. Once he's seated, he seems to steady himself. It's not like him to do that, and my heart skips a beat, because *what's coming next*?

'Look, I haven't wanted to say anything,' he mutters, his shoulders slumping, 'but . . . well, I'm just not getting any peace during the daytime.'

'Why?' I ask.

'It's Twigs,' he says.

My mouth falls open. This is about Twigs?

'You don't see what he's like, Jess,' Dad says. 'When you're out, I mean. From the moment he came to us from your gran's place a year ago he's been so noisy. He was like that at our old house, and nothing's changed since he came here. I know it's not Twigs' fault. He was used to having endless attention from your gran all day long, that's all. But I can't give that to him, and when you're at school he gets bored and . . . well, he screams.'

'Screams?'

'Yes. Pretty much non-stop sometimes,' Dad says. 'He's better if I'm in the same room with him, but I can't keep coming back to calm him down all the time. I have to work, and you know how much concentration I need to restore paintings. It's my job, Jess, and I can't do it with Twigs screeching in my ear and

41

prancing across the paints in my study.' He gives me a defeated sigh. 'Plus, at this new house, I'm fighting off complaints from the neighbours all the time. It's so unbelievably . . . *tiring*.'

I pull back from Dad, stunned. I knew that ever since Gran passed away Twigs complained loudly whenever I left the house, but I always thought he settled down.

Twigs immediately sees I'm upset, and jumps up on the sofa to be closer to me.

'Why didn't you tell me Twigs is so noisy while I'm out?' I ask.

'Tell you?' Dad lets out a long breath. 'You had enough to worry about, losing your gran. I just hoped I'd eventually get used to the noise, that's all. But I can't, Jess. Even earplugs don't work.'

I stare at Dad, see the dark shadows under his eyes. If I'm honest, those shadows have been there for months. He didn't look like that when Twigs first arrived from Gran's last year. But what's he saying? That he can't bear to have Twigs with us any more? That we have to get rid of him?

'Dad, it's not Twigs' fault!' I say, panicking. 'I'll just come *straight* home from school every day! I'll come back as soon as school ends, and—'

'No,' Dad interrupts, his voice firm. 'You've been doing that ever since your gran passed away. You've given up virtually all your spare time for Twigs. You used to go out sketching, remember? You had

42

time for friends, too, and that's the way it should be. Twigs takes up virtually every second you've got these days.'

I feel tears coming into my eyes.

'I don't need time to myself!' I explode. 'Dad, don't you understand? I *like* being with Twigs! I'm not missing out on anything! I'm not!' I'm standing now, hardly able to contain myself. 'He's missing Gran, that's all! It's hard for Twigs without her. You know it is. We have to make it happy for him, Dad! We can't abandon him. Gran's gone. It's me and you now. We're all he's got!'

Twigs, confused, nuzzles my hands with the side of his beak. 'Jess?' he says.

Dad takes deep breaths, waiting for me to calm down. 'I know we can't abandon him,' he says. 'That's not what I'm suggesting, Jess. I know what he means to you – and how much he meant to your gran as well. All I'm saying is that I need to get some peace and quiet during the day. If we could just find someone to look after Twigs during weekdays, while you're at school, that would be enough.'

Dad closes his eyes a moment, then says to me, 'I know there's nothing wrong with Twigs, Jess. He's a great-hearted bird. I'm just really struggling here. But it's not just me who's struggling. Twigs is, too. He's lonely when you're not here. He's used to Gran providing company all day long. He needs someone who can give him that sort of care and attention while you're at school.'

Dad waits for me to say something back, but this time I don't. I'm too upset. Even if we can find a place for Twigs during the day, it will be strangers looking after him. He *will* think we've abandoned him!

'I have one suggestion,' Dad says quietly. 'There's an organisation not far from here. It's called Bertrams. It's a bird charity. They take care of exotic species like Twigs. I could give them a call. Maybe they can help.'

My heart is instantly racing at the name *Bertrams*. It would be doing that anyway, given the conversation, but there's another reason – Gran told me about Bertrams. 'I visited that so-called bird sanctuary once,' she explained to me years ago. 'I wanted to see what it was like, in case anything happened to me. Bertrams is overcrowded, Jess. All the species are shoved in together. It's a horrible place. Birds die much too soon there.'

When I tell Dad that now, he shakes his head.

'Gran made that trip over thirty years ago,' he says. 'Yes, perhaps Bertrams *was* badly run then, but it's a state-of-the-art facility these days, specialising in large parrot species. I've checked and I think we should consider it – just for during the day.'

I nod but I'm not really listening any more. I'm breathing hard and still tearful. I just can't take all this in. Dad tries to put a comforting arm around me, but

I don't let him. Still clinging on to Twigs, I pull away and run upstairs.

Once I'm in my room I hold Twigs, unable to calm down.

I try to forget about what Dad's said for a while and do some sketching, but my fingers are trembling. Twigs sees that and leans against me. When I accidentally clutch his wings too hard he shrieks.

'Shush, sorry, sorry!' I tell him. 'But we're in deep trouble, Twigs. You've got to stay quiet when I'm out. You've got to!'

He gazes up at me thoughtfully, licking my palm with his funny round pink tongue. 'Jess?' he mutters. 'Jess?'

I log on to my computer and check out the Bertrams website. I discover the buildings have all been modernised and rebuilt. But what does that mean? I know Gran visited it a long time ago, but when it comes to Twigs' welfare it's her judgement I trust most.

What about Dad, though? I had no idea he suffered so much on his own with Twigs. It's unfair to let that go on, too.

Twigs doesn't leave my side all evening. He can tell how upset I am. Balancing on his tail, he keeps pressing his wings against my hands, blinking worriedly.

Around nine o'clock he interrupts my whirling thoughts by gently pecking my ear. He's letting me know how late it is.

That gets me off my pillows.

'Bathroom?' I say.

Twigs knows exactly what that means. He hops off the bed and we head along the corridor together. It's the start of our bedtime routine.

First – teeth brushing, where Twigs gets to help me by holding a yellow child-sized toothbrush in his beak towards my face. OK, he gets most of the toothpaste on my nose, but who cares? Once we've finished that, he licks a dab of spearmint toothpaste off my chin.

'Glug glug,' he says, copying the sound of water gurgling down the sink.

Afterwards I stroke his crest several times from back to front (he hates it the other way round), and splash tap water onto his wings. Only a few drops, though. Any more and Twigs screeches the house down with excitement. Tonight I'm especially careful about that.

We head back to my room and Twigs waits patiently for me to get into my pyjamas. Then, with a satisfied squawk, he jumps onto the chair and up to the wooden perch in his cage.

From there we both turn to look at a photo of Gran on the bedroom wall. We do this every night. The photo is a snapshot of Twigs leaping onto Gran's

46

shoulder. In the photo she's grinning up at him, laughter lines running like spaghetti around her eyes. Normally I find myself smiling at Gran's expression, but not tonight.

Twigs, as he does every evening, gazes at the photo intently. '*Moon moon, come down soon,*' he murmurs, repeating something in his memory from his days with Gran. Seeing her photo always brings out Gran's words. I never quite know what Twigs is going to say at these moments. 'Quiet, quiet,' he mutters tonight. 'All be well. Stroky well. Be well . . . close your eyes and sing. All be well, all be well . . . Gran is here. Gran is here.'

I stare hollowly at him. Gran was always finding reassuring words for Twigs. I'm supposed to be the one doing that now, but I can't find any tonight.

'You miss her as much as me, don't you?' I say, stroking his feet.

'*Mwaaaaaaaaaaa,*' he answers.

Turning away from the photo, I stare thoughtfully out over the garden. Twigs follows my gaze, bobbing his head at a bat skimming between the trees. When he finally turns away from the window he's nearly ready for sleep, but not quite. First I have to place a threadbare green blanket over his cage. The blanket is at least twenty years old and still smells faintly of the sweet lavender of Gran's house. Twigs has trouble sleeping without it.

47

As a last treat I give him his most indestructible toy – a rock-hard blue rubber star.

Holding it in his beak, Twigs smacks it against the bars of his cage a few dozen times. The bashing gets slower and slower as he tires until – with a *clunk* – he drops the star to the cage floor.

That's when I turn the main light off.

'Night night,' Twigs mutters in Gran's voice, letting me know he's ready for sleep.

'Night night,' I whisper back.

I get into bed, listening as Twigs toddles on and off his perch. It's the very last thing he does before dropping off. S*crunch, scrunch, thump,* I hear as he leaps between the floor and his perch. *Scrunch, scrunch, thump.* He does it more times than usual tonight. He's restless.

Eventually, with a last rustle of tail feathers – and one more fluttery jiggle of his wings – he gives a low, strangely sad-sounding whistle, stops moving altogether and falls quiet.

Silence.

When I nudge the blanket aside with my finger, Twigs' head is flopped on one side, eyes closed.

He's asleep.

Not wanting to disturb him, I lie back quietly on my bed, sinking into the pillows.

What am I going to do?

Every time I think of Bertrams my stomach twists.

It's not just that Gran would hate it. If Twigs ends up there, he won't have the one-on-one relationship he's used to. He'll just be one of hundreds of birds. Dad may not be able to give Twigs much attention during the day, but I'm sure he'll get even less at Bertrams. Poor Twigs won't even know who the new people are! He'll be confused and upset. He'll be frightened, too. He's used to being in a house with only one or two other people. Whatever Dad says, I think Bertrams will scare him half to death.

As I lift Twigs' blanket off his cage and gaze at his trusting face, just the thought of him being shoved in with people he doesn't know makes my chest ache. This isn't me keeping my promise! Gran would never have allowed anyone to separate her from Twigs, so how can I?

Six

Breakfast next morning with Dad is strained.

I find him in the kitchen in his blue dressing gown, slowly stirring a coffee. It's obvious he's worried he's upset me, and he has, so I stay on my own side of the table. As I mix Twigs' nut and fruit breakfast I can't think of anything to say. It doesn't help that Twigs is especially happy today, after seeing a robin in the garden.

'Shut up, you bacon butty!' he shrieks at Dad in delight as I go to rinse out our breakfast bowls. 'Whoo-waaa, you bacon butty!'

When Dad cringes, being blasted by one piercing *Whoo-waaa* after another, something snaps inside me.

I know I can't leave Twigs with Dad today.

I don't plan what happens next. After dressing for school and getting my bag ready I just drape Twigs' green blanket over his transportation cage. The cage is only used for short journeys like going to the vet, and it's heavy with Twigs inside, but I set off before I change my mind.

When Dad asks me where I'm going, I lie: I tell him we're having a special Pet Day at school.

Mrrrrraaaaaaaaa!

Even covered by his blanket, Twigs hates being outdoors. He complains like mad on the journey, and my arms are soon aching with tiredness.

I don't even know why I've headed towards school. I'm not sure where else to go, that's all. It rains on the journey, which is hard on Twigs. Rain scares him as much as wind. To keep him from panicking, I get soaked using my jacket to keep him dry.

As I carry Twigs inside the school building, I'm relieved that no one else has arrived in class 6B yet.

Oh. Wrong! Mrs Baldwin is at the back of the room, bending over some files. Seeing me dripping, her eyebrows arch up.

'Let me just rest a sec,' I say, realising what a stupid idea it was to come here with Twigs. 'I'll just put this cage down a minute . . . I'm sorry . . .'

'Jess, what's going on?' Mrs Baldwin asks.

I'm so upset that the whole story pours out. Twigs. Gran. Dad. Everything.

51

'May I?' While she hands me a towel to dry off, Mrs Baldwin takes a peek under Twigs' blanket.

Frightened by the journey, Twigs lunges at her. Luckily the transportation cage door is tightly shut.

'I'm sorry,' I tell her. 'He's scared by all the bumping around, that's all. It was silly bringing him in. I'll take him home again. It's all right . . .'

'No, it's not all right, Jess. It's far from all right.'

Mrs Baldwin hesitantly glances inside Twigs' cage again, and gets a beak hacking at her fingers for her trouble.

I wince. 'He didn't catch you, did he?'

'Missed,' Mrs Baldwin grunts. 'He can be a grouchy old boy, can't he?'

'It's the journey,' I tell her. 'I shouldn't have brought him in. I'll take him home . . .'

'Or you can stay,' Mrs Baldwin says.

That surprises me, and I look up. 'You mean keep him here?'

'Will Twigs stay quiet if you hang the blanket over his cage?'

'Yes. Actually, um – not for long. A few minutes at best. Basically . . . no.'

Mrs Baldwin shrugs. 'Well, I'm certain we can put up with him for a day. And if anyone complains I'll come up with an excuse. Either way, your dad gets a rest.'

'Thank you,' I burst out, so grateful that I'm almost

crying. 'I'm sorry about this. Sorry to cause problems.'

'Problems?' Mrs Baldwin gazes at me over the top of her glasses. 'You're not causing me problems, Jess Soper.' She smiles. 'Now, finish drying yourself off before you drown.'

By the time the others turn up, Twigs is out of sight in the storage room at the back of the class and my clothes have dried. Danny sees straight away that I'm upset, though.

So does Lucy. 'What's wrong?' she asks, gazing at me through her fringe.

Hearing her voice, Twigs instantly makes a menacing 'RRRRRZZZZZZZZZZZZZZ.'

It's his soldier mode. He doesn't know what the dangers are in this place, so he's getting ready to protect me.

'Ah,' Mrs Baldwin announces. '6B, Jess has a pleasant surprise for us.'

With that, she grins at me and, as if it were planned all along, brings the cage containing Twigs out of the back room.

The twins immediately run to either side of his green blanket and snatch it off.

The first thing Twigs does is puff out his chest and send out a stunning warning yowl. 'RRRRRAAAA AAEEEEEEEEEEEEEE!'

'Wow!' Hamish whispers. 'That's . . . that's a huge bird.'

'Very huge,' Angus confirms. 'We can do a lot with that. How much do you want for him, Jess?'

I shoot both of them a sharp look. 'He's not for sale.'

Twigs follows my look and gives the twins a stare to freeze the blood. 'GRAAAAAAAAK!'

'Whoa, he's a bit of a bad boy!' Hamish says, impressed. 'He's guarding you, isn't he?'

Lucy blinks, mesmerised by Twigs' sheer size. Whipping out her latest poem pad, she readies it on her knees.

Danny's the one whose eyes widen the most. A smile settles across his lips. 'Jess, he's amazing!'

'He's gorgeous,' Lucy remarks, underlining the word in her pad. 'That's what he is. *Totally gorgeous.*'

'HE'S GORGEOUS!' Twigs shrieks back at her.

When everyone laughs, Twigs gets excited by the attention. '*TOTALLY* GORGEOUS!' he screams. 'HE'S GORGEOUS! SHUT UP!'

Hearing '*shut up*', the twins fall off their chairs in hysterics.

From the floor, Angus reaches towards Twigs' cage, but soon pulls back when Twigs lunges for him. 'After my fingers, are you?' he mutters. 'Don't trust me, eh?'

Hamish grins. 'What did you expect him to do, lick you like a puppy?'

Everyone crowds around Twigs' cage after that, ogling him.

'Keep back,' Mrs Baldwin warns the twins. 'He's not something to be prodded and poked.'

'GIVE UZ A KISS!' Twigs yells at her, and Mrs Baldwin almost chokes.

'He's a mimic,' I explain. 'He says things like . . . oh, never mind, never mind.'

'NEVER MIND! NEVER MIND!' Twigs screeches. 'YOU'RE TOTALLY GORGEOUS!' he wails again at Mrs Baldwin, and Lucy giggles so hard that she's almost wailing, too.

'Just leave him alone with us for half an hour, Jess, that's all I'm asking,' Hamish pleads. 'I promise we won't teach him anything stupid.'

'No,' Mrs Baldwin says firmly. 'Twigs stays here under Jess's supervision. He's not allowed to leave this room.'

Angus leans towards the cage. 'Twigs, huh? Is that his real name?'

'Twigsy-Twiglet's his full name, and be careful,' I tell him, 'his beak's super-sharp.'

Lucy can't stop making notes. 'Can he fly?' she asks.

'No.' I say. 'Well, I don't think so. A vet said that because Twigs was stuck in a cage for so long when he was young his wing muscles are probably too stiff to ever get him off the ground. But Gran kept his flight feathers clipped anyway.'

'Hey, Twigs!' Hamish waves his hands in front of the cage. 'Talk to me! Say something!'

Angus shoves his brother aside. 'No, forget him, Twigs. Talk to *me!*'

The twins carry on like this until Mrs Baldwin settles them down and asks me to tell the class Twigs' life story. When everyone finds out that Twigs has never been outside they all go quiet.

'Never flown, never left home, never known the sky,' Lucy whispers, pausing over rapid jottings.

Right on cue, a breeze sweeps through the classroom from an open window. Shrieking with fear, Twigs buries his head in his chest feathers.

'Sorry, sorry,' Danny apologises as if it's his fault, and shuts the window.

I open Twigs' cage and take him in both arms. He likes being held that way when he's frightened – completely surrounded by my touch.

As he sits on my lap, recovering, I notice that his fear of the others is less than I expected. He's still glancing suspiciously at Mrs Baldwin, but he only seems curious about the twins, Danny and Lucy. I think I know why. It's because they like him, and he can tell. It's that simple. Just in case he changes his mind, though, I keep tight hold of him.

'Has Twigs ever met any other Moluccans?' Danny asks. 'Any of his own kind, I mean?'

'I'm not sure,' I say. 'He was taken from Seram

56

Island as a chick. Gran always told me that male cockatoos are competitive, so she avoided any contact with them.'

Danny looks surprised. 'He's been alone his whole life?'

'Yes, I think so,' I confess, feeling a rush of guilt.

Lucy is writing away. 'I love it that he talks!' she says. 'Words from a bird!' Then she stops writing, her pen poised over the page. 'Does Twigs know what he is?'

'What do you mean, Lucy?' Mrs Baldwin asks.

'I mean, does he know that he's a bird?' Lucy prods her glasses. 'If he's spent his whole life around people, maybe he thinks he's one of us. That he's *human*.'

While we're all considering that, the school bell chimes. *Dong-ding-dong* it goes, and Twigs' head nearly twists off with excitement.

'DONG-DING-DONG!' he squawks. 'Waaaaa aaaa!'

Angus creeps up so close that his hair spills over Twigs' claws. 'Hey, Twigs!' he whispers. 'Say my name! It's Angus.'

'Ffffffffff!' Twigs splurts back.

'Go on,' Angus beseeches him. 'Say my name! Say it! Say it!'

'SAY IT! SAY IT!' Twigs screeches.

As Hamish laughs, Twigs twirls his neck and blasts him with a huge friendly 'HERRRROOOOOOOO OOOOOOOO, DEARIE DARLING!'

'Oh, he's so cute!' Lucy squeals.

'Is he rare?' Danny asks. 'He *looks* rare. I'll bet he's rare.'

'Very,' I tell him. 'Hardly any are left in the wild. Moluccans have been listed as endangered since 1989. You can only breed them in captivity from Moluccans bought before that date.'

Danny shakes his head. 'People always want rare things, don't they? And look at his plumage! Even in a colourful jungle you couldn't miss him, could you?'

'Of course not,' Lucy agrees. 'He'd stand out a mile.'

'Why don't you get people to pay to stroke him, Jess?' Angus says. 'We'll take him into the playground at lunchtime for you if you like. You'll make a fortune. We'll only take fifty per cent.'

'Twigs remains right here,' Mrs Baldwin growls. 'No pranks.'

'OK!' Angus raises his hands innocently. 'We'd have looked after him, miss, honest. What does he eat, anyway, Jess?'

'Given the size of that beak, I bet it's live mice,' Hamish says.

'Twigs is vegetarian,' I tell them both, 'but he loves chewing things. Especially hard plastic.'

Mrs Baldwin leans towards Twigs. '*Coochy-coochy-coo*,' she sings out, completely surprising us, and Twigs squawks back, 'YOU'RE GORGEOUS!'

Then he spits at her.

Oh dear.

Yes, Twigs can spit when he's excited. It's not his best trait. For a moment Mrs Baldwin is too shocked to speak.

Danny rescues the situation by wiping her collar with his sleeve. 'Twigs is brilliant!' he says.

'COOCHY-COO!' Twigs screams. 'COOOCHY-COOCHY-COO!', and Mrs Baldwin has to back away as he spits at her again. He misses this time.

'Whoa!' Hamish says.

'Yeah!' Angus grins. 'He's a complete nutter, isn't he? A noisy nutter as well.'

'WHOA!' Twigs screeches. 'NOISY NUTTER! NUTTER! NUTTER . . .'

And he's off. He gets stuck on *nutter* about a hundred times. That's typical of Twigs. He's so thrilled by the new word that in the end I have to put him back in his transportation cage before he explodes in my hands.

'NOISY!' Twigs screams at us from inside. 'NOISY NUTTER! NUTTER! WHOA! NOISY NUTTER! NUTTER! NUTTER! NUTTER . . .'

And he's off again.

'He's great.' Danny shakes his head. 'I'd have him at my house, Jess, with all the trouble you're having. But my mum won't have pets, you know that.'

I smile gratefully at him, realising I'd love Twigs to be with someone warm like Danny when he's not with me.

'The solution's obvious,' Lucy says, closing her poem pad firmly. '*We* should have him. The class, I mean.'

For a second no one says a thing. We're too surprised by the suggestion.

Then Angus's eyes light up. 'Exactly!' he cries. '*Us.* 6B. At least during the day.' He glances at Mrs Baldwin. 'Can we? A class pet, miss! Wouldn't that be great?'

When Mrs Baldwin shakes her head, Hamish gives her his best smile. 'Why not, miss? Jess knows how to look after him. It'll be easy!'

'Oh, it'll be easy, will it?' Mrs Baldwin grunts. 'I don't think so. Anyhow, there's no way I'd be allowed to— Oh!'

The '*oh*' is for a teacher who's just appeared in the classroom doorway.

We all know him – Mr Ginty. Head of Maths.

He's disliked by everyone. Permanently sarcastic, he took us for equations on Monday afternoon as part of the 'experience a new teacher' initiative the school is trying out this week to add variety to lessons. Somehow, during the lesson, he managed to make us all feel stupid.

'Er – excuse me,' he wheezes, talking through his nose as always. 'It's noisy in here. Very.'

Sniffing the air as if Twigs smells (which he doesn't), Mr Ginty slicks back his straight black hair. The front is gelled up into a stiff curly quiff. He's much too old for that hairstyle, but it's obvious how proud he is of it.

'The bird's arrival was pre-arranged with me, Harold,' Mrs Baldwin says to him coolly.

Mr Ginty sneers. 'Wants an education, does it?'

Twigs is in a good mood thanks to all the attention he's receiving, so he just shrieks cheerfully at Mr Ginty.

Mr Ginty's face screws up into a pinched ugly triangle. 'What exactly is it? Some kind of squawking vulture?'

Mrs Baldwin rises out of her chair. 'Pleasant sound, isn't it?' she says.

Twigs chooses that moment to spit at Mr Ginty. It's a beautiful shot. Hits him right on the neck.

'Ugh! *Foul!*' Mr Ginty snorts. 'How disgusting!'

'SHUT UP!' Twigs tells him, and hops out of his cage. Uh-oh. I forgot to lock it, and I can see from the way Twigs is huffing across the floor that he's taken the same dislike to Mr Ginty we all have. He starts running, beak wide, straight at him.

'Get away! *Ughh!*' Mr Ginty wails as Twigs chases him around the chairs, pecking at his feet.

Mr Ginty's skinny legs wobble as he races for the classroom door. Barely making it out in time, he hides behind it. 'It's against regulations,' he whines. 'School rules clearly state that pets must not be inside classrooms.'

Mrs Baldwin strides frostily out of the room to speak to Mr Ginty. She whispers to prevent us hearing her, but we can just make out her voice through the shut door.

'Complained to the Head already, have you, Harold?' she mutters. 'Without even talking to me about it? I'm surprised you can hear us at all from Block Eight, but I noticed you opening all your windows so you'd have an excuse to come over here and moan. You know very well there's no regulation in this school about pets.'

When Mrs Baldwin returns to us, she rocks thoughtfully back and forth on her chair for a second or two. Then she gazes at Lucy and the twins.

'A few days in class with Twigs is what you were suggesting, wasn't it? Good idea. In fact, on reflection, until the end of the week sounds perfect to me. Seram Island is Geography, so we're justified there. Twigs is old so we'll call that History. Nature. Biology. Yes, I think we're educationally covered. Plenty of time for Jess's dad to get a break as well. Of course, we'll need your dad's permission too, Jess.'

'I think it'll be quite easy to get that,' I tell her, thinking of Dad wincing this morning at breakfast.

Mrs Baldwin nods. 'In that case, I'll chat to the Head during lunch break.'

Twigs picks that moment to stretch his neck and

peck a chunk out of Mrs Baldwin's pine chair. I hold my breath.

'I never did much like that item of furniture,' she notes, winking at me.

Seven

Leaving Twigs caged in the back room to rest, we all go to lunch. I take my sketch pad with me, and can't resist doing a drawing of Mr Ginty being chased.

'That's so cool,' Hamish says. 'Hold on, Angus! We can make money out of this. Let's photocopy the sketch and sell copies at the school festival this Saturday.'

'Nice idea,' Angus agrees. 'Hey, Danny, that reminds me. Last night we came up with a new argument to persuade your mum to take Kim on. How many friends has she got?'

Danny has a think. 'A few, but not that many.'

'Right,' Hamish says. 'But people like dogs, yeah? So if she gets one, they'll visit her more often. She'll have loads of friends. Tell her that.'

We come back from lunch to find Mrs Baldwin sitting behind her desk. She looks flushed, as if she's been through a minor battle.

'Well, that wasn't easy,' she says, 'but the things in life worth fighting for often aren't. The Head, you'll be pleased to know, has agreed we can keep Twigs in class until the end of the week.'

When we all cheer, she holds up her hands. '*But* if we're going to do this, there's a cost. Twigs will disrupt lessons, so your lunch breaks will be only half an hour long this week. Any objections?'

For a few seconds no one says anything. Then Hamish shrugs. 'I eat fast, anyway.'

'Me too,' Angus agrees.

'That's good to hear,' Mrs Baldwin says. 'And because birdy screeching will wreak havoc with your concentration, I'm also giving you extra daily homework for the next few days. All OK with that, too?'

This time the twins stay quiet.

Danny glances at me. 'That seems fair.'

'Mm.' Mrs Baldwin strums her fingers. 'And I think we'll require an epic poet to record the entire experience for posterity. I don't suppose we have any of those in the room?'

Lucy grins, raising her pen like an exclamation mark.

*

The rest of the day goes much more smoothly than I expect.

With Mrs Baldwin's wary approval, I place Twigs on the classroom floor and let him run free. It's a nerve-wracking moment: will he behave?

Amazingly, he does.

Not perfectly, of course. He jumps up onto a table and dive-bombs Mrs Baldwin not long after I let him out of his cage. He has a quick nibbly-nibble of her socks, too. But he seems to realise fast that she's not a threat to me, and she's able to get on with our lessons without too much fuss. Meanwhile, Twigs struts around the classroom like a prince, tasting chairs, nosily poking his beak inside bags and repeating the school bell whenever he hears it chime.

'Dong-ding-dong,' he warbles. 'Moo-mee-moo, schmiley schmile . . .'

Listening to his sing-song voice, the whole class is spellbound.

Quick learner that he is, Twigs figures out from the way she keeps constantly touching it that Lucy's poem pad is her prize possession. Off he runs with it in his beak, getting her to chase him. By the end of the afternoon he's memorised everyone's names as well – and he doesn't get Hamish and Angus mixed up, either.

'Have you noticed that Twigs never gets far away from Jess?' Danny says just before we go home. 'Even when he runs around he always stays pretty close to her.'

Angus laughs. 'Yeah. It's like he's looking after her all the time – as if she's his chick or something.'

'That's exactly it,' Lucy says. 'He keeps checking on you like you're his baby sister, Jess.'

Mrs Baldwin smiles at me. 'One thing's for sure – there's a special connection between the two of you. Twigs may be a bit of a grizzly old warrior, but he has a deeply nurturing side to him as well.'

'He's great with everyone here, isn't he?' I say proudly.

'Yes, he is,' Mrs Baldwin replies. 'But the one he's really great with is you.'

After school ends that day Danny helps me put Twigs back inside his transportation cage. I'm really grateful when he offers to carry him back to my house as well. On the way, towering over me by four inches, Danny clutches the cage in his left hand as if it weighs nothing at all.

Dad greets us at the front door in his overalls. He's covered in paint from a restoration he's working on, and I can't help noticing that he looks much less tired after a day without Twigs. He's anxious to make things better between us after our argument too, and gives me a big hug.

'Oh, hi!' he says to Danny. 'You're Jess's friend, aren't you? Come in, come in . . . really nice to meet you.'

As soon as we enter the living room I let Twigs out of his cage.

'Careful, Jess!' Dad warns, and I know what he's thinking – that Danny, never having been in the house before, will automatically get chased by Twigs in soldier mode.

Instead, Twigs hops onto his climbing frame as if Danny's always here. A few minutes later he toddles up to let Danny stroke his crest.

Dad watches in a trance.

'Swishy-swee!' Grinding the edges of his beak together – a sure sign he's happy – Twigs sheds a puff of white powder over Danny's school jacket.

'Oh, I'm so sorry,' Dad apologises, getting up for a cloth. 'That stuff gets everywhere.'

Danny grins, tickling Twigs under his chin. 'It's OK, Mr Soper. It brushes off easily. I read about it after Jess told us she had a Moluccan. The powder hardly stains anything, and it's one of the signs Twigs' health is good. You must be looking after him really well.'

Dad manages a cheesy smile. A few seconds later he's still got that cheesy smile on his face when Twigs spits in his direction.

Dad sways to one side. 'He's always doing that when you least expect it.'

Danny gives Twigs an admiring glance. 'It's a really impressive skill, isn't it?' he says. 'I'd love to be able to spit that accurately. Moluccans are good at loads of things. They're very clever, you know. Almost as smart as dogs.'

Dad blinks at Danny, staring at him as if he's likeable but mad. 'Really? I didn't know that.'

I roll my eyes – I've been telling Dad that for ages!

'Twigs spent all those years stuck in a cage with his first owner, but he's still so full of life,' Danny says. 'Don't you think that's amazing, Mr Soper?'

Again, Dad can't think of a reply.

We tell him the plan for keeping Twigs at school this week, and Dad's happy to give his permission. Actually, he looks relieved. *Good*, I think. *Maybe if he gets a week free of Twigs he'll stop talking about sending him away.*

With a yip of pleasure, Twigs prances eagerly across to Danny. He can't seem to get enough of him.

'Twigs seems so calm around you,' I say, realising I'm feeling a teeny stab of jealousy.

Danny shrugs, stroking Twigs' neck feathers. 'I'm just copying what you do around him at school,' he says.

'I don't do anything special,' I mutter.

That makes both Dad and Danny laugh.

'Jess,' Dad says, 'you and Twigs mirror each other's behaviour all the time. He'd do anything for you.'

Danny nods. 'You move and Twigs moves with you.'

'Does he?' I say, and they both laugh again.

We have something to eat together, then I head upstairs to my room with Danny and Twigs. When I show Danny a few of Twigs' favourite run-around games, he loves them. Seeing him laugh, I can't remember the last time anyone apart from me took so much pleasure in just seeing Twigs being happy.

'C'mon, I'll show you what Twigs *really* likes,' I say.

Leading Danny into the bathroom, I take him through the toothbrush game. Danny joins in, splashing tap water all over Twigs until he goes mental, squawking non-stop.

'Watch out, you'll drown him!' I laugh, but Twigs is loving it, his screams raising the roof until I shush him.

After his soaking, Twigs sits in the crook of Danny's arm, drenched but happy.

A frown creases Danny's face. 'Hey, we can't leave him like this. He's soaking wet. Have you got a hairdryer?'

'You're not serious?'

'You don't think he'll like it?'

'Er . . . I've never tried.'

Danny smiles. 'So let's find out!'

I fetch my hairdryer and nudge it onto a low setting. Then I stop. 'Oh, no, he'll hate it. It'll be like being outside in the wind. He'll be scared.'

'But he's inside, and he knows that,' Danny reassures me. 'Let's try it.'

I hold the hairdryer a long way from Twigs and switch it on. He can't believe it at first. Squawking anxiously, he tells me to *shut up*.

Then he goes quiet. Ever, ever so quiet. The warm air from the hairdryer gently streams over his feathers and he cautiously spreads his wings.

After that he closes his eyes. Keeping them shut, he makes a few happy mouse-like *yips*.

Those yips become squeaks that slide downward into something quieter until, finally, Twigs falls totally silent.

'It must be the warmth of the hairdryer,' Danny whispers.

'What do you mean?'

'He comes from a tropical climate originally, doesn't he? Somewhere with warm winds. This probably feels like the home he never knew.'

As I keep the hairdryer pointed at Twigs he's soon dry, but he doesn't want me to stop. He leaves his feathers exposed to the max.

And as the minutes pass new noises emerge from him. I thought I'd heard every sound Twigs could make, but I've never heard these ones before. Shivers of pleasure they are, pierced with small whoops, low and sweet, and tiny high cries, like a chick still in the nest.

'He's . . . I think he's *singing*,' Danny says.

And he's right. It's something like singing, anyway. A kind of hum. Puffing out his breast, Twigs can't stop. The noise builds and builds until even Dad comes upstairs to see what's going on.

When my arm gets tired of holding the dryer, Danny takes over.

'He looks so calm, doesn't he?' Dad says, standing at the door and shaking his head in awe. 'I wonder what's he's thinking.'

I've no idea what Twigs is thinking, but they're happy thoughts, anyone can see that. And when Danny switches the hairdryer off, Twigs stays in that happy, warm place. Turning his neck as if he's still feeling the hairdryer, his head bobs gently up and down like a boat on a river.

His beak is parted, too, but there's no sound.

'Silence,' Dad says, spellbound.

When Danny leaves, the sun is setting. He's silhouetted against it as Dad joins me to see him off. The evening is bright, with white puffy clouds bunched like cushions against the chimneys.

'I think everything is going to work out fine for

Twigs,' Danny tells me, and the way he says it, with a smile on his face and sounding so certain, I nod. For that brief moment, Danny makes me believe it.

He heads off, his bag slung over his shoulder, and the last thing that follows Danny down the street is the sound of Twigs trilling at him through the front window.

Eight

Next morning – as I carry Twigs back into school for his first full *official* day in class with us – I meet Danny outside the house. Given how heavy Twigs' cage is, he's agreed to help me carry him into school for the week, while Dad picks me up in the car each afternoon.

'HERROOOOOO, DEARIE DANNY!'

Danny waggles his fingers at the cage. 'Hello, Twigs! How's it going? You looking forward to kissing Mrs Baldwin?'

Twigs grinds his beak happily. 'WHOO-WAAAAAAA!'

*

As soon as we make it into class I let Twigs out of his cage. I expect him to be nervous, since our classroom is still a fairly new space to him, but he doesn't seem to be. He potters around, cheerfully stabbing at the walls.

Later that morning we have to leave Twigs in his cage and head off to Mr Ginty's room again for Maths. The first thing Mr Ginty does, for no reason at all, is split the twins up. He spends the rest of the lesson with his sweaty back to us, writing numbers on the board and shaking his head whenever he hears a peep out of the distant Twigs.

'I'm recording the noise from 6B,' he informs us. 'I'm sure the Head will be very interested when he discovers the decibel level.'

The twins stiffen, but they know we'll all get detention if they argue with Mr Ginty, so instead they turn the lesson into a game. *'Sir, sir, can you just explain this sum a bit more? We don't understand.'*

Mr Ginty can hardly punish them for asking questions about what he's teaching us, and it's a thing of beauty to watch Angus and Hamish co-ordinate which stupid question to ask next from across the room.

'Hasn't Mrs Baldwin taught you any of this in class?' Mr Ginty growls at one point, and it's obvious he's fishing for ammunition to use against her.

'We covered this fully at the *beginning* of the year,'

Lucy says coolly, and right on cue Twigs lets out a screech: *RAAAAAAAAA!*

When we return to 6B, Mrs Baldwin has some maps out for us. 'Right, Geography,' she says. 'Let's do tropical climates. What weird and wonderful place on earth could we study, I wonder?'

'Seram Island, where Twigs is from?' Danny suggests, and Mrs Baldwin smiles.

We spend an hour learning about Seram Island and the hot, steamy province of Maluku in Indonesia where almost all of the last wild Moluccans live. At the end of the lesson Mrs Baldwin allows us a short break to play with Twigs. 'Only ten minutes, though,' she says. 'Then let's go to the class computers and see what we can find out about other endangered bird species.'

Hamish reaches straight into his school bag. With a sly glance at Angus, he says to Lucy, 'We've brought in a treat for Twigs. Bet you can't guess what it is!'

Lucy shrugs. 'Some nuts?'

'Nah.' Hamish tosses a white furry bundle towards Twigs. 'A baby guinea pig!'

Both Lucy and I nearly have a heart attack until we see it's just a soft toy.

'Boys!' Mrs Baldwin warns them.

'Sorry, miss,' Hamish says, snatching the toy back before Twigs can reach it. 'We did get something for him, really.'

And this time – as Angus reaches into his bag –

there's a big change in Twigs. His tail shoots straight up.

I know that reaction. It means he's smelling food – something tasty – but I've never seen his tail perk up quite this high before. He sniffs the air, his neck jerking wildly.

Angus slowly pulls out a red fruit shaped like a lumpy pear.

'Papaya!' the twins whisper together.

I've never heard of it, and I don't think Twigs has either, but once he gets a proper smell of the fruit he hops up and down, unbelievably excited. He's so keen to get at it that he squeals like a baby.

'EEEEEEEEEE! AAAAAAAAAAAAAAAaaaa!'

'It's a fruit that grows in hot places like Seram Island,' Angus tells us, holding the papaya away from Twigs. 'We've got an Asian shop near us and . . . Hey!'

Twigs has snatched the papaya out of his hand. Darting off with it into a corner, his beak slams into it like a demented road drill.

'*Ewww,*' Lucy moans as the full rich scent of the papaya hits us.

It's not a pleasant smell, but it's obvious that Twigs loves it. With greedy joy he rips open the papaya's skin, gulping down chunk after wet chunk. Pink juices and black pips squirt everywhere.

While Twigs is guzzling the fruit, the twins bring

out another tropical plant. It's a leafy green vegetable this time, called alfalfa. Twigs gobbles it up almost as fast as the papaya.

'He's never had many treats,' I admit. 'Gran was only on a pension so she used basic nut-and-dried-fruit pellets. Dad and I carried on with them because, well . . . they're nutritious and cheap.'

'Hey, check this out, Twigs!' Angus says.

'EEEiiiiiiiiiiiiiiiiiiiiiiiiiiiiiiiiiiii!'

Twigs almost chokes with excitement as Angus casually throws a Barbie doll towards him.

'It's broken and our little sister Hannah never plays with it any more,' Hamish says to Mrs Baldwin before she can object. 'Twigs might as well have it. You said he likes plastic stuff, Jess.'

As soon as he sees the Barbie, Twigs spits out the last of the alfalfa in his eagerness to get at it. 'ROOOOOOOOOOOOO!' he wails, jumping on it like a giant budgie. 'SWISHY, YEAH!'

Clutching the Barbie in his right claw, he toddles off to a corner of the room. The doll's head seems to be just the right size to fit neatly into Twigs' beak. Snorting with excitement, he's just getting in a few fierce dagger blows when Mrs Baldwin chases him down. They start a tug-of-war over the Barbie, which Mrs Baldwin – surprisingly – wins.

'Return this to your sister,' she demands, handing the doll back to Angus.

'Why?' he asks, genuinely puzzled. 'It's broken, and she's got loads of others, miss.'

'It's *hers*, that's why, and you didn't ask her.' Mrs Baldwin folds her arms. 'And I'll be checking with her that she gets it back, so you'd better make sure she does!'

Twigs soon forgets about the Barbie, and the rest of the morning is . . . well, fantastic.

Why? Because Twigs enjoys himself so much. And, for once, it's got nothing to do with me. He likes everyone in the class. He can't stop burbling and chatting away. Watching him, I realise with surprise that he's nowhere near the home-loving cockatoo I believed. Gran's quiet life kept Twigs isolated so much that I thought he'd find it hard being in a noisy place like a classroom.

Not true. He's happy here. He really doesn't mind new places or strangers as long as they accept him.

At lunchtime the twins insist on looking after Twigs on their own while the rest of us go to eat. When we come back, Twigs has learned a new phrase: 'ANGY AND HAMMY ARE BWILLIANT!'

Mrs Baldwin has also pinned up a portrait of Twigs. It's one I brought in this morning. Hanging over her desk, it captures the moment of surprise yesterday when the twins first pulled the blanket off Twigs' cage.

While everyone looks at that, a chaffinch outside the classroom sings out a *trill*. Hearing it, Twigs cocks his head on one side and repeats the call exactly.

No, not exactly. Better. More perfectly. An even purer set of notes. Just as there's no British bird species to touch Twigs for looks, none of our native birds can make his variety of sounds either.

'He likes the company of other birds, doesn't he?' Danny says – and as soon as the words are out of his mouth I sit up straighter.

Yes, I realise. Twigs does like the company of other birds – but what chance has he really had to *be* with other birds? All Gran and I ever offered him is a view from the window.

'Twigs hasn't ever seen another Moluccan cockatoo,' I say. 'It's true what Lucy said before – he probably thinks he's the only Moluccan in the world.'

Everyone falls quiet, taking that in.

Finally Danny leans forward in his chair. 'Are there, you know, any Moluccans we could take him to see?'

Mrs Baldwin won't let us use the classroom computers again until a double period of English is over, but the first chance they get, the twins dive straight for them.

'Gurney Zoo is only an hour's car ride from here,' Angus reports back after scanning Google. 'They've got . . . hold on . . . cockatoos and parrots. Let me just check . . .' His fingers fly across the keys. 'No, I don't think they've got Moluccans.'

Hamish taps the screen. 'Yes, they have. Look! Two adults. A pair. Male and female. Whoa!'

'WHOA!' Twigs screeches back.

We all gaze expectantly at Mrs Baldwin.

Exploding with laughter, she shakes her head. 'Sorry. There's no point looking at me like that. There's not a hope of me borrowing the school minibus for Twigs without getting permission from all your parents. We'd need written consent from each one of them. And even if you all remembered to get that, I'd have to ask for the Head's permission, too, and I'm in enough trouble with him for keeping Twigs till the end of the week as it is.'

We don't reply. We just keep looking at her.

'OK, fine.' She grins. 'We'll create a letter of permission together. Tomorrow is the only possible day we could do it. Take the letter home tonight, get your parents' permission *first*, and if you all do so and bring your signed letters in tomorrow morning, I'll ask. But don't get your hopes up. There's very little chance the Head will say yes.'

Nine

After school Danny rushes off to spend as much time with Kim as he can. I'm just watching him run out of the school gates, and waiting for Dad to turn up, when Lucy appears beside me.

'Hi, Jess. Can I talk to you about something?'

'Sure,' I say.

'It's something *private*,' she whispers, patting my arm in that slightly possessive way she has. 'Why don't you come over to my house after you've taken Twigs home?'

An hour later I'm knocking at her door, wondering what she might mean by *private*.

The first person I meet is Lucy's mum. She's a bigger version of Lucy, with even frizzier hair. 'Extremely nice to meet you,' she says formally, her tone so like Lucy's that I can't help smiling.

She packs us upstairs with glasses of chilled lemonade and once we're in Lucy's bedroom I have a good look around. I'm expecting unusual decorations, but it's a completely standard room except for loose scraps of Lucy's verses pinned to the walls, and hundreds of volumes of poetry. The poetry volumes cover shelf after shelf.

'Valerie Worth,' Lucy sighs, stroking one. 'She wrote a poem about a safety pin once. It's brilliant.'

I notice there's an old teddy bear sitting in the middle of her bedspread.

'Do you still sleep with your teddy?' Lucy asks me, not even slightly embarrassed. When I tell her no, she shrugs. 'Oh, you should,' she says. 'It's really comforting. Have a seat.'

Once I'm in a chair, Lucy wastes no time. 'What do you really think of my poetry, Jess?'

'Sorry?' I say, caught off guard.

'You've heard enough of it recently to form a very clear opinion,' Lucy says.

When I don't answer right away, Lucy nods. 'I see. You're not sure how to reply. Are you afraid of hurting my feelings? Well, don't worry. Bad opinions don't bother me in the slightest. Besides, Mrs Baldwin likes me to recite my poems in class these days, but it's obvious people think they're a bit stupid sometimes.'

From her pinched lips I see how much this matters to her.

'Oh, Luce,' I say, suddenly realising how vulnerable she is. 'That's not true. They – we – do like your poems.'

'No need to lie,' Lucy mutters. 'I know people mostly just laugh at them. I don't care. It doesn't matter, but . . . well, you know . . .' her chin drops '. . . I suppose it does matter a *tiny* bit. I'm not totally tough as nails.'

She fiddles with a loose poem that's lying like a stray, flat animal on her desk.

'Luce, I think it's great that you write poetry all the time,' I tell her honestly.

'You really think so?'

'Yes.' I mean what I'm saying, but I can see that Lucy doesn't believe me.

She fetches a ham sandwich out of her lunchbox. 'I've got one left over,' she tells me. 'Mum always makes plain sandwiches, no trimmings. She's fantastic, but her sandwiches do lack imagination. Do you want some?'

When I say no, Lucy nods and chews the sandwich in little random bites – as if deciding moment by moment the most poetic way to do even that.

Then, with a slightly forlorn breath, she taps her poem pad. 'Poetry is a tough profession, Jess. We poets live at the point of being crushed all the time, you know. The fate of most real professional poets is total neglect. They generally die of starvation.'

I raise my eyebrows. 'Why? Because no one buys their poems?'

'No.' Lucy stares at me as if I'm an idiot. 'Because they get so transported by their own words that they forget to eat.'

'Oh . . . of course.'

Lucy strokes another poem that's lying face-down like a deserted beast on the floor of her room.

'It's well known that ninety-nine per cent of poets are entirely ignored and neglected during their lifetime,' she tells me. 'I'll probably end up that way – another dead poet. I doubt I'll last another ten years, the way I'm being neglected.'

She sighs again, looking around at the jottings all over her walls. 'Sometimes,' she says in a supremely sad voice, 'when I sit down to think of a subject no one else can possibly have been bothered to write about – like a blob of dirt on a path, or perhaps an everyday object like a pen nib, or a curtain rail, or the rusted metal door of a fridge – I wonder if I'm wasting my time. I really do.'

I smile to encourage her.

'Right now, I'm interested in poetry about general household goods,' she says.

'What do you mean?' I ask.

'You know – cutlery, vacuum cleaners, cupboards,

floor tiles, that sort of thing.' Lucy twirls her fingers. 'Poems about them aren't easy to find.'

'Really?'

'Yes, really,' she tells me, deadly serious. 'Really, really, really. I'm halfway through what I call my *salty snacks* series, too. Poems about peanuts, pork scratchings, Hula Hoops, Pringles, that sort of thing. Poets have unjustly neglected them. Do you want me to make one up for you right now?'

I grin. 'How about a crisp poem? I've never heard a poem about those.'

Looking pleased, Lucy thinks for a while, her eyes turned to the ceiling, then clears her throat and comes up with this:

'Oh, crisp,
What is it like inside your snug little packet?
Do you fear the light?
Do you fear the bite
Of hungry lips?
Do you have nightmares of gnomes
Poking stone fingers
Into your dark crinkly homes?'

'Nice! I like the gnomes,' I say, and Lucy's face brightens.

'I must admit I didn't totally improvise that one,' she tells me. 'I thought up the hungry lips line last night. I'm trying to mix tragic elements back into my verses again. The main problem is that I don't have a lot of true-life tragic experiences to draw on yet.' Her shoulders drop. 'Until those tragedies come along I'm having to wring the last drop out of every single bad thing that's ever happened to me. Luckily, I've eaten a lot of crisps and they're not too tricky to write about.' She frowns and bites her lower lip. 'Do you *really* like the crisp poem, though, Jess? Be honest.'

'Yes, I do,' I tell her. 'It's great!'

She leans forward. 'In that case, how do you feel about helping me with a poetry event at school?'

I blink. 'An *event*?'

Lucy stands up, briskly setting off around her room. 'Yes. I've been thinking of reciting poetry in the playground at school. Something fairly low-key, obviously.' She flings out a hand. 'I wouldn't expect you to read out any poems, Jess – just stand beside me when I do. I've got to be brave enough to start reciting in public at some point if I'm going to be a poet. I can't just hide in class for the rest of my life.'

'It's a great idea,' I say. 'Of course I'll help.'

'Fantastic!' she cries, her voice filled with relief. 'That's so what I was hoping you'd say!' Her eyes burn eagerly. 'Shall we dress up for it? I was thinking we could cover ourselves in poems. You know, pin paper to our clothes filled with verses. They can blaze there

87

like badges of beauty, expressions of love. We'll sort of become living, walking rhymes.'

Inside, I'm worried now. 'Um . . . actually . . . er . . . Luce . . .'

Then I see she's laughing. 'It's OK, Jess. I'm only joking about dressing in poems. I know it'll be hard enough to stop the Year Nines and Tens making fun of me without that. But still . . . I'd really like to do it. Will you just stand next to me, so I'm not on my own?'

When I smile and say yes, Lucy can't contain her excitement. 'I knew you'd help me,' she says.

'What about trying some of your old Fluffy poems on the Year Twos?' I suggest. 'You can't go wrong with bunny rabbits!'

'I've never thought of doing that.' Lucy walks across to her bookcases. 'Here they are.' She runs a finger across a shelf entirely covered in pink poem pads. 'Look at them all!' she says, grinning. 'It's hard to believe I could write so many poems about a single rabbit, but I loved that happy little bunny.' She flicks through the first pad, giggling and shaking her head. 'The Fluffy poems aren't very good, obviously, because I was only a kid when I wrote them, but maybe you're right and the littlies *would* like them. Will you have a look and tell me if they're too awful to read out loud?'

'I'd like that,' I tell her. 'Give me some to read at home.'

Selecting one of the pink Fluffy pads at random,

Lucy dumps it in my hands. 'There, that's settled then,' she says. 'When will you start reading the poems?'

'Tonight,' I tell her. 'I can't wait.'

I do start reading Lucy's Fluffy poems that evening, and a lot of them *are* funny enough to entertain Year Twos. Some of them are very good, too, considering that Lucy was only five when she wrote most of them. By the seventeenth one, though, Twigs, perched beside my shoulder, shrieks, 'GRAAAAAK!'

'Not into them, huh?' I mutter. 'How about I read just a couple more?'

Twigs doesn't look very enthusiastic, but I decide I will anyway. I stroke his neck feathers. 'This is poem number fifty-six,' I tell him. 'It's called "I Love Fluffy":

'Little feet,
Titchy toes,
Twitchy, twitchy, twitchy nose,
My love for you grows
And grows
And grows.'

I show Twigs how the writing gets bigger and bigger towards the end.

'Mwwwwaaaaaaaa.' He shakes his wings and gives me a sympathetic glance.

As a reward for putting up with the extra Fluffy poem, I take him for an especially long brush and splash in the bathroom, followed by Danny's new hairdryer trick.

Shortly after that, Dad pops into my room to see me and I get him to look at the consent form Mrs Baldwin needs for the trip to the zoo. Dad signs the form, but doesn't leave. He wants to show me an internet enquiry. It's from a man called Alfie Parks.

'He's telling everyone on the large bird websites that's he's looking for a Moluccan to buy,' Dad says, 'but I thought I'd ask him if he'd like to help take care of Twigs.'

My heart sinks when I hear the enthusiasm in Dad's voice. I was hoping a week's break from Twigs would change his mind but, thinking about it, that was stupid of me. How could one week be enough when Twigs is so noisy whenever I'm gone?

I glance at Alfie Parks' details, but not too closely. 'I'll check him out later, yeah?' I manage. 'Is that all right? I'm . . . I'm busy right now.'

'OK, Jess.' Dad nods slowly. 'Later is fine.' He goes to leave, then lingers by the door. 'I know how hard it is for you to think of Twigs being left with a stranger,' he says, 'but will you try to get used to the idea? I'm not trying to make Twigs' life miserable, Jess. I promise we'll find a solution that's best for him, too, but we need to do something.'

'OK,' I murmur, and give him a little smile, but as Dad tramps downstairs I'm suddenly scared again. Why does Dad keep talking about leaving Twigs with a stranger? He'll be really unhappy! He'll hate it!

I'm chewing a pen top, still trying to think of what to do, when Danny rings my mobile. He can barely get out his words.

'Jess . . . a man . . . he rang the Fletchers . . . he rang . . . and . . .'

'It's Kim, isn't it?' I say. 'What's happened?'

After another snatched breath, he finally comes out with it: 'They've sold her, Jess.'

'What? The Fletchers? You're kidding!'

Danny's voice almost disappears. 'No. It's true. A family called the Nesbitts want a guard dog for their house. Kim's a pedigree Rottweiler. They've offered a decent amount of money for her. I always knew the Fletchers would sell Kim on eventually, but . . .' His voice trails off.

'Oh, Danny.' I hold the phone closer to my ear. 'The new family won't stop you from seeing her, will they?'

There's a long silence this time. 'I'm not sure. The Nesbitts say all my playing with her has already made Kim too soppy and friendly. They're telling the Fletchers I've made their job of toughening her up much harder.'

'Toughening her up? What do they mean by that?'

Danny's voice shakes down the phone. 'I don't know. But they want her as a guard dog, remember?' He suddenly bursts out, 'That's the last thing Kim should be! She scares way too easily! It's not fair to her, Jess. She'll hate it. She won't be able to do it!'

I hold the phone tightly. 'What can I do to help, Danny?'

'Nothing,' he mutters. 'Nobody can do anything. It's too late. The Nesbitts took her this morning. But they've been planning to buy her for weeks, apparently. The Fletchers say Kim was even training with them last week. No one's telling me what the training involves, but I don't think I'm ever going to be allowed to see her again.'

I try to comfort Danny, but he won't calm down, and I don't blame him. If Twigs was taken from me, I'd be just the same.

'I did something dumb tonight as well,' he murmurs. 'Really dumb. When I got the news, I found out where the Nesbitts live and went over to their house. They wouldn't answer the door so I shouted through their letter box. I only asked if I could sometimes take Kim for walks, but as soon as she heard my voice Kim started barking like mad. She was going crazy, scratching at the front door to get to me. It was terrible.'

We talk a while longer and when Danny finally

hangs up, I take a deep breath and lean back against my pillows.

Then I reach out for Twigs. I pull him tight to my chest, and shiver. *Yesterday*, I think, *Danny had Kim beside him, as close as me and Twigs are now. Tonight, just like that, Kim's gone from his life. That's how fast you can lose things.*

Will the same happen to me and Twigs? Because that's what I'm really worried about. I'm scared about leaving Twigs with strangers, but if I'm honest there's another reason I'm scared, too. I'm scared that a new person might really like Twigs. Because, if they do, daytimes might not be enough for them. What if they want *more* of him in the evenings? And what about weekends? Given the way he feels, Dad might agree.

I'm frightened that once Twigs is out of the house I'll never get him back.

Ten

Next morning, as we walk side by side towards school with Twigs, Danny doesn't say a word. He's too upset about losing Kim.

'Any more news?' I ask, watching him closely.

'The Fletchers rang me this morning,' he says tightly. 'They're going to ask the Nesbitts to let me see Kim. That's all they can do now, they say. They're not promising anything, but they're going to try to get me a weekly visit. That's something, isn't it?'

'Of course it is,' I say, and the little look of hope that brings to his face nearly makes me cry.

We walk along in silence after that, because we both know a weekly visit isn't much, and when we get to school I'm glad when Lucy starts off the day by distracting us with a couple more verses from her *salty snacks* series. Then, after a double Maths lesson (a proper one with Mrs Baldwin this time, no Mr Ginty!) we do Geography, History and French.

Twigs likes the unusual-sounding French words. 'BONJOUR!' he shrieks, long after we're finished. 'BONJOUR, MONSIEUR LAFAYETTE!'

In the afternoon Mrs Baldwin permits him a free run around the class, and Twigs is off at once, darting between desks, pecking at anything chewable. Each day, we notice, he seems happier and more comfortable in class.

During another break, I show everyone one of his favourite games. Giving Twigs a cross-eyed stare to get his attention, I whisper it: '*Copycatcopycatcopycat.*'

'COPYCATCOPYCATCOPYCAT,' Twigs repeats, instantly breathless with excitement.

'What are you doing, Jess?' Angus asks, as they all huddle round.

'Watch,' I say, giving Twigs a hard stare.

Twigs – his blue eyes bulging – matches my stare.

Then I give my head a quick waggle.

Twigs does the same.

I say, 'Waaa.'

He says, 'Waaa waaa!'

I clasp my feet together. He brings his claws together.

I flap my arms. He flaps his wings.

I jump. He jumps.

'GIVE UZ A KISS!' I say, and 'GIVE UZ A KISS!' he squawks back – and we do, stretching our necks out for a quick lip-touch.

As Lucy chuckles, I lift my left foot off the floor and hold it in the air.

Twigs copies me – raising his left claw.

He freezes in that position, staying totally still.

Danny has seen me play this game over at my house before, but the rest of them are bewildered.

'What's Twigs doing with his foot up like that?' Hamish asks.

'He's waiting for me to move,' I tell him. 'During copycat we stay still for as long as we can. Twigs loves playing it. It's always me who moves first. His balance is incredible.'

Eventually I move my tired leg, and – '*RAAAAAA!*' – Twigs screeches happily.

Yet again, he's outlasted me.

In the final mid-afternoon break, Mrs Baldwin asks me to run an errand for her, and I'm just on my way past the Year Five classes when I spot a boy staring at the floor near the entrance to the canteen. I can see why he's staring. There's a huge chocolate sponge cake on the floor. Who knows where the cake came from, but the boy can't believe his luck and quickly bends down to pick it up. As soon as he touches it, a massive orange spider leaps onto his hand.

'Urgggg!' The boy shakes it onto the floor and runs off screaming.

Grinning their big, wide, identical grins, the twins appear from behind a door. 'It's on a touch-sensitive wire,' Angus explains. 'We're trying to get as many people as possible before the day ends. Six so far. Very realistic, don't you think? It bites, too. Not real fangs, obviously. We can get you one if you want, Jess.'

They look surprised when I say no.

The rest of the day goes smoothly at school, but once I'm home I get a big surprise, and it's not a good one. I've barely tucked Twigs into my bedroom when Dad's bundling me back inside the car.

'Where are we going?' I ask, as he jumps into the driver's seat.

'You'll see,' he tells me.

He won't say anything else, and after a twenty-minute journey we end up outside a large flat-roofed building. I haven't been feeling worried till now, but as soon as I see the sign above the main gate my mouth gapes wide in shock.

BERTRAMS

the sign reads.

A SANCTUARY FOR EXOTIC BIRDS.

'Don't panic,' Dad reassures me when he sees the look on my face. 'We're only paying a visit to see what they're like. They're willing to provide a weekday fostering service for Twigs. I've spoken to the manager already, but we haven't committed to anything. I've been promised Twigs will get lots of individual attention. I just want you to see what they're offering.'

My stomach is churning as Dad parks the car.

The manager of Bertrams strides out to greet us. *Andy Dekany*, his nametag says. He looks very efficient in his crisp blue suit as he sweeps us into the reception area.

'Hello, you're Jess, aren't you?' he says. 'I understand you'll need persuading that we're a good day-care option for Twigs. That's OK. I'm happy to show you around.' He looks like he's in a hurry, but he smiles indulgently at me as he checks his watch. 'Shall we go inside?'

We're led into the corridors of the main building. Andy Dekany walks in front, talking to me over his shoulder.

'Your dad's told me how important Twigsy-Twiglet is to you, Jess. You'll find we've improved out of all recognition since your grandmother visited all those years ago.'

I nod warily, but relax a little once we're in the primary area where the birds are kept. It's clean, airy and well maintained, with lots of windows. Dad's right.

Bertrams is no longer the grim place Gran described. All the enclosures are new. They're big, modern and roomy.

The squawking, squonking and hooting from the big birds hits me like a delicious wall of sound as soon as we walk into Enclosure A.

'We have over two hundred avians housed at Bertrams,' Andy Dekany tells us. 'They're all exotics of one kind or another. Mostly big, colourful parrots: Amazons, African greys, chattering lories, etc.'

I nod, fascinated. I know plenty about the big parrot species – the *talkers*, as bird fanciers call them – though I'd prefer to watch them on wildlife films than see them stuck in captivity like this.

We turn a corner, and I suddenly spot a Goffin's cockatoo. They're smaller than Moluccans, and nowhere near such good mimics, but they have lovely distinctive red markings on either side of their beaks.

Dozens of parakeets and macaws are housed at Bertrams as well and, as we pass them, I have to admit that the birds are not mistreated. They look healthy. I can tell they're being given plenty of room and food.

'Cuttlefish and vegetables, nuts and millet as required,' Andy Dekany says. 'A varied, I would go so far as to say *adventurous*, diet. Being mostly ex-pets, all the birds get human company every day as well. Mated birds are allowed to pair in separate enclosures. That means they get privacy. And all the birds have visits not just from the general public coming into the centre, but from handlers working at the facility, too.' He smiles. 'We cater for much more than their basic needs here, Jess.' From the smooth way Andy Dekany rattles everything off, I can tell he's given this speech a hundred times.

We're near the end of the tour when I ask, 'How much time do the birds get to spend alone with a person they love?'

That question surprises him.

'Erm, well, *love* . . .' He laughs uncomfortably. 'Who knows what that word means, eh? I'm not sure we can say the birds here are individually loved. The staff are busy. But they care for the birds, of course.'

Dad avoids catching my eye.

I slow right down, forcing Andy Dekany to do the same. 'What games do you play with them?' I ask.

The question obviously annoys Andy Dekany. 'We generally haven't got time for that, Jess. Bertrams is a charity. We mostly look after birds that are unwanted. We find permanent homes for those we can. Or we provide temporary foster care, which we'll do for Twigs if you agree to it. A rare bird like Twigs will be a real star if he comes here. A *celebrity!*' He smiles at me, as if I'll be impressed with that. 'Twigs will bring in plenty of new visitors to the centre. And that, in turn, will bring in much-needed money. Bertrams is expensive to run.'

Ah, I think. *So that's why you're giving up your personal time for this little walk-around with me. You want Twigs.*

'What about your older birds?' I ask. 'How do they cope here?'

'Mm.' Andy Dekany looks irritated now, glancing at Dad as if to say, *Do I really have to answer all these questions from a kid?* When Dad doesn't step in, Andy Dekany reluctantly turns back to me. 'I'll admit older birds are generally harder to keep happy. They have more quirks – odd habits picked up over a lifetime. They can be tricky to deal with.'

He waffles on then about age categories and staff-to-bird ratios, and when I listen closely I realise he's trying to hide the fact that most of the older birds are on their own at Bertrams. People rarely take them. It sounds like many end up being isolated, especially the ones that for one reason or another don't get on well with other birds.

Andy Dekany shifts away from the subject as fast as he can, rabbiting on. It's as we're nearing the exit that I spot something.

A flash of blue.

It comes from an enclosure in Block C. There's a bird inside. A bird impossible to miss once you look in her direction.

A macaw.

And not just any macaw.

The macaw. A hyacinth – not just the largest macaw, but the largest of all the parrot species. Bigger even than Twigs.

She's so dazzlingly beautiful that she instantly takes my breath away.

'Rrrrrrrr, crrrrkkkk,' she squawks, shaking out her immense wings.

Mandy Walnut, the name plate on the wall above her head says, and somehow that name fits her.

Dad's never shown an interest in any birds apart from Twigs, but even he gives a little gasp when he sees Mandy. Anybody would. She may have a funny name, but Mandy Walnut isn't a funny-looking bird. She's majestic – pure royal blue, with a yellow eye as proud as an eagle's.

I can tell Andy Dekany is trying to hurry us on, so I resist him and pull Dad inside the enclosure.

As soon as she sees she has company, Mandy's beak drops open in a look of utter surprise.

'Hello,' she says. 'Hello. Hello. Hello. Hello. Hello.'

At first it makes me grin, hearing that one word, but when she keeps on saying it I step closer.

'Hello,' Mandy squeaks, dropping her head submissively. 'Hello. Hello. Hello. Hello. Hello. Hello. Hello. Hello.'

A cold feeling shivers through me.

'Ah, I see you've discovered Mandy,' Andy Dekany says, and it's obvious from his expression that he was hoping we'd miss her. 'Mandy hasn't fitted in that well, to be honest. We look after her, but she has behavioural issues. She can be aggressive sometimes, and she's not that keen on other avians. Lunges at the staff. Noisy . . . erm . . .'

'Hello. Hello. Hello. Hello. Hello. Hello.'

Dad frowns. 'Why does she keep saying that?'

Andy Dekany shrugs. 'How can anyone figure out why a bird repeats one thing rather than another? It doesn't mean a thing, in my opinion.'

'Yes, it does,' I whisper, moving closer to Mandy. 'Can't you see? She's saying it because when someone walks in, *hello* is the one word guaranteed to get her more attention.' I swallow, turning to Dad. 'She's desperate to be close to someone – for any human company. Look at her, Dad! Look at the submissive way she's bowing her head. She's dipping it *below her knees*! No bird like her should ever feel the need to lower herself that way to a stranger.'

'Don't touch!' Andy Dekany growls as I reach out to Mandy, but I ignore his warning. What's wrong with him? Can't he see that this bird isn't going to bite someone who approaches her in a friendly way?

When my hand finds her, Mandy turns her head against my fingers. She does it over and over. I can tell she's feeling sheer relief.

'Hello. Hello. Hello. Hello. Hello.'

'Hello,' I say. 'Hello, Mandy Walnut. Hello to you.'

'Hello,' she says, more softly now, gratefully raising her head to stare at me, a bit of pride coming back to her. 'Hello. Hello.'

As I stroke her long wings, a bleak feeling rushes though me and I turn sharply back towards Andy Dekany. 'Mandy had a single owner most of her life, didn't she?'

He hesitates, reluctant to speak.

'Didn't she?' I insist.

'Er . . . I think that's right,' he admits. 'I'd need to check her records to be sure, but yes . . . I think you're correct about her having lived with a single owner. Some birds with those kind of backgrounds don't do so well here.' Clearly having had enough of me, he turns to Dad. 'Mandy's an unfortunate case, Mr Soper, but we're still hopeful of finding a permanent home for her. She's just . . . well, we need to find the right owner. It's not always easy with the older birds.'

I let Mandy press and rub the soft feathers of her face against my fingers. 'No,' I murmur. 'It's not, is it?'

Not long after that, we go. It's horrible leaving Mandy behind, but what choice do I have? Dad's hardly going to take her on as well as Twigs.

On the way back in the car he's tight-lipped. I can't tell what he's thinking.

'It's not just that Twigs won't know anyone at Bertrams,' I say, determined to make absolutely sure he understands. 'It's other things, too. What about run-arounds and games? Who'll be there to play those with him? Who'll be there to do *anything* special with him?'

'I know,' Dad says hoarsely, and I can tell from the way it comes out that it's not only me who's been affected by seeing Mandy Walnut.

'You were right, Jess,' he goes on quietly. 'Bertrams . . . is not the place for Twigs. OK, we'll forget about bird charities, and look exclusively for a private owner with a proper home instead. Someone who lives close to us, obviously. Someone who likes Twigs as well – *really* likes him,' he adds when my face stays flat. 'I'll place an advert on the classified internet bird sites. We're bound to find someone if we look hard enough.' He glances worriedly at me. 'And while I do that, will you check out Alfie Parks? I know you don't want to look at his details, but he seems really good to me.'

'OK, I will,' I murmur, but even as I say it my heart is sinking. It's not Alfie Parks I want Dad to be reminding me about! I want him to say he'll try a little harder with Twigs himself first!

As soon as we're back home, I traipse upstairs to see Twigs. A couple of hours later Dad knocks on my bedroom door. He wants to show me an advert he's written.

Loving elderly Moluccan cockatoo — Twigs (50). Likes nibbling, but is affectionate. Bit noisy, but quietens down once he knows you. Needs a home during weekdays (9-5 only) as his current owner is no longer in a position to look after him during the day. Will transport to you and take Twigs back daily within a reasonable distance. Twigs is a head-turner and in perfect health. A great talker . . .

I finish reading the note, then hand it back.

'I know it's not the whole truth,' Dad admits. 'I haven't said anything about the constant shrieking, but Twigs doesn't do that with you, so if we can find someone who enjoys playing with him that might not be a problem.'

Inside, I can't help it, I'm screaming: *If YOU enjoyed playing with him, we wouldn't need to do any of this!* But I understand that Dad shouldn't have to do that, and at least he reassures me before leaving my room that it will only be during school hours that I have to give Twigs up to someone else, never weekends. Even so, thinking about Twigs having to cope with Alfie Parks or any other stranger makes me go cold.

As soon as Dad's gone, Twigs scrunches up against my side. 'Th . . . th . . . th . . .' he says, nudging me for a kiss.

'OK,' I manage, bending down to his face.

After kissing him I drag him onto my tummy, keeping back the tears.

Will Twigs be able to cope with a new daytime owner? I don't know. A house is better than Bertrams, but what if we can't find the right person? At least Bertrams has set standards by which they treat every bird. If Twigs ends up in Alfie Parks' or another person's house, how will I know they're being good to him? How can I even think about sending him to a stranger's home when I know it's the last thing Gran would ever have done?

Eleven

As I walk into school with Danny and Twigs next morning, there's still no news about Kim. It makes the journey to school a solemn one, but at mid-morning break Mrs Baldwin has the best surprise in the world waiting for us.

'Thanks to all your signed consent slips, the Head has miraculously said yes,' she announces. 'It means I have permission to take everyone, including Twigs, to Gurney Zoo to see the Moluccans today.'

She bursts out laughing as we all go crazy. In fact, as we bundle into our coats and I pack Twigs into his transportation cage, I'm so happy that I can hardly find the voice to thank her.

'No need,' she whispers eagerly in my ear. 'I can't wait to see myself how he reacts!'

We get to the zoo easily enough in the school minibus, but while Mrs Baldwin is parking she sends the twins in to check the entrance cost and they discover a problem: visitors can't bring in animals.

'We can't tell Mrs Baldwin!' Angus cries. 'If she knows, she'll have to drive us back.'

'There must be something we can do!' Lucy says. 'We can't leave now!'

Danny takes off his rucksack. 'This is almost empty. Do you reckon you can get Twigs inside and keep him quiet long enough for us to slip through the entrance, Jess?'

I think about it. 'Maybe. It's worth a try.'

We head back to the car and, while Mrs Baldwin is paying the entrance fee, I hang back and ease Twigs inside the rucksack. 'For safekeeping,' I tell Mrs Baldwin, when she gives me a curious look.

Twigs isn't comfortable in the darkness, but, with the twins chatting loudly to cover up his grumbling, we just about manage to blend in undetected at the entrance along with the other zoo visitors.

The parrot house containing the Moluccan cockatoos isn't far inside. As we enter it I hastily loosen the rucksack.

Unzipped, Twigs shoves his head out so fast he

almost breaks my wrist. His neck springs up like a rocket, his face twisting in all directions.

'Quiet,' I shush him.

For some reason, even though I'm still trying to hide him, I'm grinning like a madman. I feel incredibly excited. But where are the Moluccans? All we see at first are parakeets and cockatiels.

Then Hamish spots them – and, oh, they're beautiful! Two creamy-white adults. Sitting side by side on a branch in their own fenced-off area, they take my breath away. Their bodies are touching, their crests flat against their heads – a sure sign they're relaxed.

As we crowd closer to the metal wiring of their enclosure, one bobs its neck and stares at us warily. 'Graaaaaak,' it mutters.

The female, I realise. She's slightly smaller, with a characteristically brownish tint to the iris of her eye. I've always loved studying these tiny differences between male and female Moluccans, but I've never had a chance to see them in the flesh. The male – black-irised – doesn't consider us worthy of serious scrutiny yet. He just tilts his head sideways.

The female thinks differently. 'Mrrrrrrrrvvvvvvvvv,' she rasps, followed by a piercing hoot and the kind of fierce blow-your-brains-out screech we're all so familiar with from Twigs.

We all gasp. And laugh.

But that's nothing compared with Twigs' reaction.

As I swing the open-topped rucksack towards the Moluccans, he goes very still inside the bag at first.

Super-still.

Then – like an exploding missile – he's struggling with every bit of strength he has to get his shoulders fully out. Bobbing like a maniac, his head looks about to snap off.

'Lift him up so he can see them,' Danny murmurs – and I do.

'Higher,' Angus says, and I stretch my arms far enough to put Twigs on the same level as the pair of Moluccans in the enclosure.

The male spots Twigs first. He makes a wheezy high-pitched squawk.

Hearing it, Twigs' crest shoots straight up in amazement, then actually stretches backwards over his crown. His shoulders wobble so hard it looks like he's trying to behead himself.

'It's OK, Twigs,' I soothe him, feeling him shake. Is he frightened? I'm worried he is, but I soon realise it's not fear he's feeling. He just can't believe what he's seeing. He emits a questioning, timid *squeak* as he spots the female.

'WHOA! YEAH!' he pipes – and the two Moluccans in the enclosure scream his words straight back.

'WHOA! YEAH!'

Blasted by that, Twigs screws up his eyes and wriggles in my hands. '*Gggggggguuuuuuuu.*' He's so desperate to get closer to them that he sounds like he's drowning in his own excitement.

Lucy stares into my eyes. 'I didn't really think he'd recognise his own kind,' she says, 'but he does, doesn't he? He does.'

Mrs Baldwin motions with her fingers. 'Let him go, Jess. Let him meet them in his own way.'

When I free Twigs he tumbles and spins from my hands to the ground. But he's immediately on his feet again, swivelling his neck up.

He just stares up at the Moluccans at first, simply stares and stares. He's so beside himself with wonder and disbelief that his tail's a blur, whipping around like a flag in a storm. In fact, he's shaking so hard that I can feel his crest fanning me, and the next moment he leaps, more like a monkey than a bird, straight from the ground onto the wire mesh of the enclosure. Clinging desperately to it with his claws, he scrambles and bites his way up to the Moluccans.

I've seen Twigs insanely excited before. I've seen him squeal with emotion when I've been away all day. I've seen him topple over furniture in his desperation to greet Gran when she came back from shopping. But I've never seen anything like this.

'HERR-HERRRR-HERR—' Twigs chokes. He's too emotional to get the word out. Finally he steadies his neck and crows it: 'HER-HERR-HERROOO OOOOOOOO!'

I'm weeping, and so is Lucy.

'HERROOO! HERROOO! HERROOOOOO
OO! HERROOOOOOOOOOOOOOOOOOO!'

The welcome pours out of him. He can't stop saying it. Breast heaving, his screeches are so loud you'd think he must surely be in pain but, whatever Twigs is feeling, it's as far from pain as anything can get.

'HERROOOOO! HERROOOOOOOOO!' He just keeps calling and calling it, and at last the female yells it back.

'HERROOOOOOooooooooo! YAYAYAYAYA!'

Twigs does a double take. Stiffens in astonishment.

YAYAYAYAYA?

What kind of noise is that? It's a Moluccan sound, clearly, but not one Twigs has ever heard or made before.

Whatever the female is saying to him, though, deep in his bones, Twigs understands it because he goes completely motionless. Total shutdown of his beak: *crunk.*

Lucy is writing as fast as possible in a poem pad, her tongue sticking out in concentration.

But Twigs is unaware of Lucy. I think he's unaware of us all in that moment. For Twigs the world just seems to have stopped.

That *yayayayaya* has done something to him. It's as if the female has said something his mother or father never had a chance to say, something important and

113

reassuring, and I don't know quite how to describe it, but Twigs just . . . settles.

He goes utterly still. His feathers quiver and fall back smoothly. Then, like a windswept sheet slowly falling down from a height, his whole body shivers once – deliciously – and when he opens his beak again and breathes out it's almost like he's taking his first breath.

I sense the female has given Twigs a gift – something only another Moluccan could offer him – but we don't know what the gift is. It's for Twigs alone.

Then she approaches him.

She jump-hops down from her branch until she's almost touching him through the wire mesh.

Then they do touch.

Twigs makes contact.

It's just his crest against hers, and a clumsy scrape of beaks, but it's something.

And the most amazing thing is that the male of the pair stays back. It's so unlike a male Moluccan to do that. I've read about every detail of Moluccan behaviour, and normally the male in a mated couple will be fiercely protective of his pair bond.

But this one remains on his perch, watching. It's as if he knows this isn't a battle for courtship, but something much more important – Twigs' right to basic companionship with his own kind. Which, if I'm honest, isn't just something his first owner Harry

Smith starved Twigs of. Without meaning to, Gran did as well. And so did I.

We can't stay long. Twigs' screams of sheer joy at seeing the other Moluccans alert a zoo keeper. He isn't happy when he discovers we've smuggled Twigs in. Mrs Baldwin reasons with him, but the twins react angrily when the keeper grabs her arm to lead her away.

'Get off our teacher!' Angus yells at the man.

'And leave Twigs alone as well!' Hamish yells even louder. 'Can't you see he just wants to talk to the other Moluccans? What's the matter with you?'

That gets us escorted out by no fewer than three keepers, and it takes all of Mrs Baldwin's diplomacy to calm the situation down.

I barely hear what anyone is saying, though. I'm too busy cradling Twigs. He's not affected by the argument with the zoo keepers. He's in some other, more perfect, place.

I don't bother putting him back in the rucksack. I just carry him to the minibus, my head full of that eerie *YAYAYAYAYA*, and seeing again in my mind the deep dip and rise of the female's neck as she graciously offered that sound to Twigs.

On the drive back to school, I slip Twigs back into his transportation cage to keep him safe, but leave it on my knees so he can see out of the windows.

He's incredibly quiet. Not a peep out of him. No whistles. No grumbles. No moaning as we hit bumps in the road. Not a single screech. His crest is flat, his features so composed that I can't tell what he's thinking about at all.

That hushed mood lasts the entire journey. Twigs just stays in a better place, lost inside his own private spell.

Lucy has a poem pad on her lap, but instead of writing in it she only watches the cars and lorries streaming past us on the roads. Eventually she says:

'Divided by a fence, they start;
Two birds filling a yearning heart,
And much too soon they part.
By their tender wings he is fanned;
Voices together, they take their stand,
Twigs' crest rises, like a little hand.'

No one says anything after that for a while.

Finally Angus turns in frustration to me. 'I was a total idiot back there!' he apologises. 'It was stupid to shout at that zoo keeper! Twigs would have had longer with the other Moluccans if I hadn't. Sorry, Jess. Stupid, stupid.'

'Me, too,' Hamish grunts. 'I should've kept my mouth shut.'

'Twigs still got to see the other Moluccans,' Mrs

116

Baldwin reassures them. 'That's all that matters.'

Lucy reaches across to stroke Twigs' crest. 'That *yayayayaya* was almost a kind of kiss, wasn't it?' she says to me in a whisper.

As we drive through the school gates Danny winds up the front passenger window. All this time the window has been open, a stiff breeze blowing into the minibus, but not once has Twigs complained. With a small shock, I realise something else – he was *outside* when he met the Moluccans. He should have been scared. But he was too excited to even think about it.

As Mrs Baldwin parks the minibus it's Hamish, sitting on the back seat, who says, 'Twigs was happy when he saw them, wasn't he? He was so happy.'

'He still is,' I whisper. 'Look at him.'

Turning off the minibus engine, Mrs Baldwin glances in the rear-view mirror at all of us.

'Twigs didn't just find out that other Moluccans exist today,' she tells us. 'He got to learn about himself as well. His appearance. How he moves. Everything a Moluccan *is*. The great gift you all gave him is the realisation that he is not alone. And if you're a smart creature like Twigs – one who thinks about things, one who wonders – that's probably the most important gift of all.' She pauses. 'It's a good thing you did today, even if you did sneak him in. I'm proud of you all. And boys – you were right to shout at that zoo keeper. He was an idiot.'

*

It's almost the end of the school day by the time we get back to class. Even so, there's still time for Twigs to play. I encourage him to run around, but I quickly realise he's only doing it to please me. His mind is elsewhere. When I pat my knees he immediately hops up onto them and lies down, his head dreamily balanced on my thigh. He's unbelievably quiet. So quiet that Mrs Baldwin keeps glancing across to check on him, along with everyone else.

'Is he all right?' Lucy asks me. 'I've never seen him like this.'

'I think so,' I whisper. 'He's just super-chilled. Super-happy.'

'Of course he is,' Hamish says, stroking Twigs' crest. 'He's just had an interesting day, and now he's thinking about it, that's all.'

'It wasn't just an interesting day,' I say. 'I think Twigs just had the best day of his life.'

That evening in my room Twigs' tranquil, serene mood continues. Dad is amazed by how quiet he is. Twigs doesn't want to play his usual bathroom games. He's not interested in his starfish or the hairdryer. He doesn't even complain when I read him one of Lucy's poems called 'In My Jim-Jams, Watching Fluffy'. He just seems to be waiting for something.

I don't know what that something is until dusk, when the garden birds start roosting. Over a period of about twenty minutes they pack the two leafy beech trees lining our garden – sparrows, robins, starlings, finches – all calling out to each other in their own way. A pair of magpies begin a hissy argument with a blackbird, chasing it off.

Twigs follows everything, concentrating on every sound, occasionally joining in, but mostly just listening.

Then he makes a request. He taps the windowpane with his beak.

I realise he wants it open.

A cool wind is blowing, and at first Twigs won't put his head out. He glances at me for reassurance. But he doesn't wait for that reassurance. He finds it in himself. Pushing his big face forward, he shyly opens his eyes and murmurs, 'Chrrrrrrrr.'

A sparrow is close by. Hearing its own call, it hesitates.

Twigs gazes at me, blinks, then gives a humorous cock of his tail before staring out of the window again.

The garden birds eventually retire to their nests, but Twigs doesn't leave the window. He stays on my pillow next to it, letting the breeze ruffle his feathers.

'Night night,' he murmurs at one point, sounding so exactly like Gran that I can almost see her there. 'Night night, Daddy,' he says softly. 'Night, Ooocy.

Night night, Danny. Night night, Angy and Hammy. Night, Gran. Night night, Jess. Nighty-night.'

Placing one wing against my shoulder, he lies next to me. I feel him twitching from time to time, and realise he's reliving his memories of the day. He doesn't want to go to his cage later, either. He's not interested in doing any of our usual night-time routines. He just wants to stay quietly beside me. And when he finally falls asleep, new noises comes from him that fill our room. Peaceful little murmurs they are and, at one point, so softly whispered that I barely notice it, a single tender *yayayayaya.*

Twelve

When Danny and I carry his cage into school next morning, Twigs doesn't once complain about the jostling. Perched behind Gran's green blanket, he simply trills away. He's not irritable. He's not complaining. He's just quivering and singing in gentle bursts.

Danny grins, taking a peek under the blanket. 'What's he doing that for?'

'I don't know,' I laugh. 'I just know he's happy!'

The trilling is something that started as soon as Twigs woke this morning. Quiet little brush-stroke warbles pour out, with hardly a breath between, making him sound more like a cooing dove than a cockatoo. 'Brrrrrrrr, brrrrrrr, brrrrrrr.'

'He won't stop doing it,' I tell Danny. 'He's never made sounds like it before.'

It's Friday, which means Twigs' last day at school, and the fuss over him begins as soon as we arrive in class.

The twins are waiting inside the door to shower him with macadamia nuts and sunflower seeds. Mrs Baldwin gives Twigs a tickle under his beak and a *coochy-coo*. Lucy brings out a fresh juicy papaya, which Hamish hides in his pocket, sending Twigs in a crazy run around the class to steal it from him. Angus is online from the moment he arrives, checking out where there might be other Moluccans we can take Twigs to see.

Oh – and there's another surprise. My gift to the class this time. Last night, while Twigs was asleep, I woke up and spent an hour doing a sketch of him meeting the other Moluccans.

Twigs, of course, is the celebrity of the day. Lucy starts us off with a poem about his wings. Twigs tells her to *shut up* after she finishes, but he does it so sweetly that we all laugh. All morning he's ridiculously cheerful and carefree. Barely making any screeching noises, he just plays with his toys, burbling away. 'Bluuur-blaar-swishy-swee-bonjour.'

The classroom window is open and, when Angus

tuts and closes it, Twigs surprises us all again by complaining. Head-butting the window pane, he rattles his wings until Angus re-opens it. Then he tips his tail up in gratitude and excitedly presses his big face into the breeze.

It's just before lunch that Twigs murmurs his first *yayayayaya*. The new noise the female Moluccan taught him floats in the air like the beginning of a song, and we wait to see if Twigs will say it a second time. He doesn't, and when Hamish tries to encourage him by whispering a *yayayayaya* of his own, Twigs dashes straight across the room to peck his leg.

'Hey, Twigs!' Hamish yanks his foot back. 'What was that for?'

Twigs shakes his tail at him and potters off.

I grin at Hamish. 'I reckon *yayayayaya* is a private thing, just for Moluccans. I think he'd rather we didn't say it, that's all.'

During lunch Danny gets a worrying text message. It's from Kim's old owners, the Fletchers. Apparently Kim has run away from the Nesbitts' house, and no one knows where she's gone. Danny turns away to call the Fletchers, and I'm just wondering what to do myself when Lucy corners me near the gym. She looks like she's about to make an announcement, and she is. Her face is shining.

'The time has come, Jess.'

'The time for what, Luce?'

'Our poetry event!' she gushes. 'After yesterday with Twigs I woke up and thought, *Today's the day to be brave.* I know it's risky – the older kids might laugh if they hear us – but shall we?'

'Yes, c'mon, let's do it,' I say and, taking her arm, stride with her towards a raised area in the west corner of the main playground.

Am I worried about looking stupid? You bet. But so is Lucy. Clinging to me, she's putting on a smiling face, but from the way she keeps prodding her glasses it's obvious how nervous she is.

She's way too frightened to recite any of her own poetry at first. Instead she squeaks out a verse called 'The Eagle' by Alfred, Lord Tennyson – a favourite of hers.

She tries to keep a low profile while she does it, but of course there's no way she can do that for long. A couple of older boys soon overhear her.

One Year Ten shouts, 'Everybody! Hey! Check this out!' so loudly that even some of the teenage boys who can never be distracted from their football wander over to see what the fuss is about.

'Don't worry, you'll be great!' I whisper in Lucy's ear,

squeezing her hand. 'Do one of your improvisations. They'll love it!'

She swallows, then raises her chin and makes herself stand up straighter.

'Hello everyone,' she says in a quavering voice as a small crowd gathers. 'I'm Lucy Daniels. I'm, um, a poet, and I would like to create some verses with you. I improvise – make up poems based on suggestions. Would . . . would anyone care to give me a subject?'

Gazing at the intimidating faces of the older kids surrounding us, I'm suddenly scared, but now that she's started Lucy is braver than me. Far braver.

'Anything,' she says. 'Give me any subject. I don't care what it is.'

A Year Nine girl folds her arms. 'Carpet fluff,' she says flatly. 'Do a poem about carpet fluff.'

Lucy looks skyward for a moment, then begins, but her voice instantly dries up.

'I'm sorry,' she apologises. 'Let me . . . let me start again.'

A Year Eight boy laughs. 'Carpet fluff *and* a mouse,' he says. 'A mouse and its *hair*. Do all of that in one poem if you're that good!'

'And love,' the original Year Nine girl adds, her voice oozing sarcasm. 'Mix in some love, too.'

Snorts of laughter echo around the playground, and for the first time I see Lucy tremble.

'OK,' she says, licking her dry lips. 'Carpet fluff . . . a mouse . . . hair . . . love . . . all together.'

There's silence, and I try to hold Lucy steady, but faced by so many older students she hesitates again. Seeing that, they snort dismissively and begin to wander off.

'Wait,' Lucy squeaks. 'Please wait.' But her voice is so strangled that only I hear her. 'I have it!' she whispers.

'I love you, said the cushion to its chair,
I love you, said the mouse to its hair,
I love you, said the carpet to its fluff,
I love you—'

But it's too late. Nearly all the kids have walked away. Lucy keeps reciting, but when she realises no one is listening she shrinks, hunches into herself and . . . *stops*.

Oh no. No, no, no, no. I can't let this happen.

I look in my bag. There it is – the volume of Fluffy poems.

Grabbing Lucy's arm, I guide her to an area of the playground where the Reception, Year One and Year Two kids are playing. A few older students follow us, including the sarcastic Year Nine girl, no doubt hoping to embarrass the two of us, but there's nothing I can do about that.

With Lucy standing in a kind of numb shock beside me, I open the pad at random.

'OK, poetry time,' I say to the littlies milling around the swings. 'These poems were all written by a kid your age about her rabbit, Fluffy. Pay attention. Hey, you lot by the climbing frame, I'm talking to you! Are you ready?'

Lucy seizes my hand. 'I can read them if you like, Jess,' she murmurs, but one look at her and you can tell she's nowhere near recovered enough to read anything.

I narrow my eyes at the youngest kids. 'This first poem,' I say, glancing down, 'is called "Fluffy is Snuffly".'

The sarcastic Year Nine girl explodes with laughter. Hearing that, my tongue refuses to move for a second, but then I just say it:

'Fluffy, Fluffy, Fluffy
Why are you so soft and snuffly?
Why are you so warm and luffly?
Fluffy, Fluffy, Fluffy.'

Finishing, I clear my throat, making a sort of mad *buzzzzzzzing* sound. I don't dare look up at anyone. Only a crazy person would look up. I can already hear the laughter of the watching Year Nine girl and a few Year Tens. Something about their sneering laughter makes me really angry, though, and I bring the next poem in the pad close to my face.

'This is poem number forty-two,' I say. 'It's called "Fluffy Eats Her First Carrot".'

'Oh, juicy orange carrot,
Friend of mine,
Let me bite you,
So I feel fine!'

I look up when I finish this time. There's a pimply sixth former in front of me. He's grinning cheesily, and I grin back. Hmm. I know I'm about to become known forever at Ashcroft High as Fluffy Rabbit Girl – but there are worse things.

I decide not to look at those laughing. In fact, I don't look at the older students at all. Instead I focus on a Year Two. She's a glossy-haired Asian girl with enormous brown eyes. She looks like she can't wait for me to start the next poem, and in my mind she becomes a true admirer of rabbit poems. *Fan of Fluffy*, I decide to call her and, from that point on, when I need encouragement, it's her I look for.

I read three more poems in succession, ending with 'Fluffy Sees Another Bunny, and it's Beautiful'.

I smile at Fan of Fluffy. It's become automatic now, that smile. My mad Fluffy Rabbit Girl smile.

Beside me, I realise that Lucy's really emotional.

128

She's holding my hand tightly. Does she want me to stop? Unsure, I look at her. She gently prises the poem pad out of my hands and opens it up.

'The next poem,' she says, 'is called "Don't Make Me into Rabbit Stew".'

Lucy chuckles, then begins to read. I haven't told you how good at reading poetry Lucy is, have I? She can bring any poem to life. Reading each line, her voice strengthens, and when her tone changes and she tells the younger kids several poems about a time when Fluffy was sick, she slows down as well, and even some of the older kids stop laughing.

With a note of defiance Lucy says the last line of the final poem again: 'FLUFFY'S POOR SICK BREATH IS ALMOST A MURMUR . . .'

She stresses that last word – '*murmurrrr*' – then she flings her arm out, lets the *rrrrr* float on the wind with a flourish like a ribbon.

And I look at her.

And Lucy is *radiant*. I can see how joyful she is. Then, as she reaches for my ears and tilts my head down like a lamp, I see that she's not the only happy one. A little boy and two young girls – including Fan of Fluffy – are sitting cross-legged in front of us.

The boy is gazing worriedly up at Lucy. 'Did Fluffy get better?' he asks.

'Yes,' Lucy answers, with a grin.

'And does she still like carrots?' asks Fan of Fluffy.

'Oh, yes.' Lucy hesitates. 'Well, Fluffy passed away some time ago now, but, yes, she adored carrots her whole life. She never, ever got sick of them.'

The rest of the little crowd of Year Two gather round us, and Lucy takes down their names and classrooms, promising to deliver photocopies of the Fluffy poems to their teachers.

Fan of Fluffy is the last to leave. She presses Lucy's arm. 'Do you have any more? Poems, I mean?'

'Yes,' Lucy says. 'Lots and lots.'

'I like them,' the little girl tells her. Then she scuttles off, calling brightly behind her, 'Oh, sorry! I have to go! I forgot to eat my lunch!'

Lucy is in a daze as she guides me – or am I guiding her? – back to our classroom.

A few older kids stifle laughter as we pass, but I don't think Lucy even hears them.

The sarcastic Year Nine girl isn't one of those laughing, though. She looks amused as we pass, but she gives Lucy a tiny nod of respect. 'Not bad,' she says.

'The younger ones,' Lucy whispers to me as we walk away and cross the school hall. 'I should have tried them before, Jess. Thank you. Here.' She looks shy as she removes a poem near the end of the Fluffy poem pad and hands it to me. 'I know it's only a silly verse about a rabbit, but it's yours to keep forever. An original. You can pin it to your dress,' she jokes.

'Thanks,' I laugh, on a strange kind of high. 'I don't know what to say.'

'You don't need to say anything,' Lucy says. 'I'll leave it for you to read later. It's about the day Fluffy made a friend when she visited another rabbit hutch.'

'Great. What's it called?'

Lucy grins. '"When Fluffy Met Tufty-Wufty".'

Once we're back in class Mrs Baldwin helps us investigate the history of Seram Island, Twigs' original home. While we study, Twigs is set free from his cage to wander freely around the class. That keeps him cheerful enough, but I'm in such a floaty mood after the poetry reading that I miss something.

The animal, I mean. The big dog stealthily approaching Twigs.

There's a door at the back of our classroom. It leads out to the public playing fields beyond the school. Today is warm and, since Twigs is now comfortable with light breezes, the door is open. Not much, but enough.

Even so, there still shouldn't be any real danger. Why? Because it's only Kim. It's only playful, lovely, adorable Kim. She must have come here to find Danny.

Except that something about her has changed.

131

She's more alert. More . . . aggressive.

Her hackles are up. *The Nesbitts have been training her*, I remember.

Thrusting her nose through the door crack, the snarl she gives Twigs is loud enough to freeze my blood.

Thirteen

Twigs can't escape. He's out in the open, bumbling about in the middle of the classroom.

Danny, seeing Kim, shouts, 'Hey! What are you doing?'

Ignoring him, Kim flashes past me, Lucy and the twins. Before any of us can stop her she's looming over Twigs, panting like a wolf. This isn't the Kim I met. It's obvious that the Nesbitts' training must have completely confused her.

Twigs swivels around. He knows about dogs because Gran had a friend who always brought her bull terrier over, but he's never been threatened by one. I expect him to scuttle off, try to get away. Instead Twigs completely surprises me. He lifts himself up on his claws, whisking up his peachy crest super-high. Then – sweeping his wings outward like a bat – he gives Kim a thunderous 'HRRRRRRRRAAAA!'

And rushes at her.

That's right. Unbelievably, in a crazy blur of feathers, he charges straight at Kim.

It's incredible to watch. Jiggling his wings, spitting and throwing his head from side to side like some kind of insane vulture, Twigs runs at her, showering white powder like a snowstorm.

We're all so amazed that we stand there, frozen.

So does Kim.

A second ago she looked menacing, but not any more. Stepping back, she gives an unconvincing growl.

It's her training, I realise. This isn't the real Kim. *They've* taught her that growl.

Danny tries to grab Kim's collar, but she's so scared of Twigs that she runs to a corner of the classroom. From there she tries another half-hearted growl.

Twigs isn't having any of that. He growls back, twice as loud. Then, with a screeched, 'GALA-GALA-GEENY!' he's suddenly chasing her around the room.

Kim yelps, loping away. All her aggression is gone. She looks like the big scared puppy she truly is. A few seconds of being pursued is all she can take, before her pink tongue flaps between her teeth like a surrender flag. Soon she's making other hopeless whining noises, and creeping towards Danny – whose arms open for her – until, with a clumsy leap, she flops like an enormous goldfish right into his arms.

Her weight brings them both crashing to the classroom floor in a heap.

Hamish shakes his head. 'Amazing!' He gazes in awe at Twigs. 'Did you ever see him do anything like that before, Jess?'

I'm too stunned to reply. But the answer, of course, is no. Stuck in houses his whole life, Twigs has never once had a chance to show how brave he is. But what's even more interesting is what he does next. Twigs could easily press on with his attack, but he doesn't. Seeing how frightened Kim is he stops, and heads back to me.

Danny is still on the floor. He tenderly strokes Kim's flank. 'There, there,' he says, whispering in her ear as if no one is here but the two of them. 'You've come a long way, haven't you? I know you weren't really going to attack Twigs. Of course not. You went a bit mad for a second, that's all. Thought you were supposed to go for him. Those Nesbitt people have made you all confused, haven't they?'

Kim whines at Danny's touch, burying her head against his tummy. Barking plaintively, she tucks her quivering nose out of sight.

'Danny, is this your dog?' Mrs Baldwin asks, puzzled.

He shakes his head. 'No, she isn't, miss. She should be, but . . . she's . . . someone else's.'

I fetch a towel from the backroom. Draping it over Kim's back, I gently tuck it around her shivering hind legs.

'Thanks, Jess,' Danny whispers.

Kim trembles and glances with fresh anxiety at Twigs. She's obviously worried he's going to attack her a second time. Then, with a great sigh, as if she's too weary to care any more, she just slumps across Danny's knees and shuts her eyes.

Mrs Baldwin lets the emotion in the room settle down, leaving Danny piled on the floor next to Kim's gangly legs. It's ages before he stops stroking her and glances up.

'She followed me,' he says, and there's a real sting of anger in his tone. 'All the way into school she followed me. What are the Nesbitts doing to her that she'd run all the way here to get away from them?'

Twigs hop-jumps towards Kim. Hearing the clickety-click of his claws on the hard classroom floor, Kim cringes with fear. But Twigs isn't trying to frighten her. He sends out what I can only describe as a kind of tweet.

'Weeeeeeeeeiiiioooooooooooooooooooooooooooooooooooooooo . . .'

The *oooo* part goes up and down like a police siren.

It's the purest of sounds, a rising note that sails sweet and high like a piccolo and descends like a sad flute. It ends on a tone so low and deep that although Twigs' beak is still open, his tongue vibrating inside, we can't hear it any more.

Which is confusing, until I realise the sound isn't aimed at us. It's not meant for human ears. It's aimed at Kim's much more sensitive dog ones.

I don't know what the note tells her but, once it's over, and Twigs shuts his beak, Kim cautiously glances up at him, much less frightened.

'Nutter,' Twigs says to her, but so amiably it sounds like a compliment.

After that Twigs bumbles across the room, wedging himself against my legs. From there he stares thoughtfully up at me and back to Kim, sending out occasional waves of reassuring *eeee*s and *oooo*s.

It's obvious how exhausted Kim is. She looks bowed down with worry – not at all like the pup I saw playing so happily with Danny only a few days ago.

Twigs toddles over to stand between Kim and the door. When a teaching assistant from Class 9F pops her head around the classroom entrance to ask Mrs Baldwin a question, Twigs warns her back with a few warning *graaks*.

'What's Twigs doing?' Lucy asks me.

'He's guarding Kim,' I say. 'He does the same for

me all the time, especially when I've been arguing with someone.'

'But no one's arguing.'

'Twigs picks up on lots more than that,' I tell her. 'He's sensing something about Kim we can't even see. He's telling us she's in real trouble.'

Mrs Baldwin can see that the last thing Danny wants is to be parted from Kim and, since it's nearly the end of the school afternoon, she lets them stay together at the back of the room.

Then, since it's Twigs' final day in class, she abandons all pretence of squeezing in a last lesson and we just spend time with him. Kim stays shyly curious behind us with Danny, while the rest of 6B gathers around Twigs for a final session of play.

As we surround him – and I watch Twigs jump-hopping, lifting up his neck to kiss everyone – I realise something: that he's completely happy in this class. It's not only me Twigs can be comfortable with. He likes other people as well. It just has to be the *right* other people – ones who accept his ways.

Twigs spends the last ten minutes before the bell goes happily bashing a plastic T-Rex against Lucy's desk until he's satisfied it's completely destroyed.

Then the moment comes when everyone has to say goodbye to him.

Luckily, it's not too gloomy because Mrs Baldwin asks if I'll bring Twigs in his cage to the school festival tomorrow. The school festival is a twice-a-year event where each class 'shows off' the best work they've done during the year to parents and anyone else interested in Ashcroft High's activities.

'I want you all here bright and early to help me set up our stall on the football field, remember,' Mrs Baldwin reminds us. 'No later than nine o'clock. That includes you, Twigs.'

When the bell dong-ding-dongs for going home, the twins can't wait to find out what's going on with Kim, but their mum is picking them up for cross-country running practice across town, so they can't join Danny as he takes her back to the Nesbitts' house. Lucy has an errand to run as well, but she gives Danny an anxious glance as she's leaving.

'Don't worry,' I whisper to her. 'I'll go with him.'

I ring Dad to let him know I'll walk home with Danny today, and as I leave I can hear Danny on his mobile, telling his mum what's happened. Afterwards, he takes gentle hold of Kim and leads her out of the school gates.

Heaving Twigs along in his cage, I catch up with him.

'It's a long walk to the Nesbitts' house,' Danny warns me. 'You don't have to come.'

'I want to,' I tell him. 'Why don't we go somewhere Kim enjoys before we take her back?'

Danny likes that idea, and between us we take turns carrying Twigs as we head with Kim to the river. The river is more a trickle running at the back of a housing estate than a real river, but it's quiet and at least there are sticks to throw on the bank.

We sit quietly on the grass for a while, surrounded by white and pink daisies. Kim hardly leaves Danny's side. She rubs her nose up against his legs and buries her head in his hands. Occasionally Danny throws a stick for her and with huge *woofs* Kim lopes away to fetch them back, but she never runs far. She stays as close to him as she can.

'She likes this place,' Danny says, staring across the water. 'There's hardly ever anybody else here but us. It's where we always come if there's time.'

Kim drops her head on Danny's lap.

I brush my fingers across the surface of the river. 'What are you going to do?'

Danny tosses a stone into the water. 'What *can* I do? Take her back to the Nesbitts, of course. They'll probably go mental if I do anything else. They might even take it out on Kim.'

It's nearly sunset and, since the weather is calm, I chance taking the blanket off Twigs' cage so he can look around. He does, checking out a few trees for roosting birds, but not for long. He's more concerned about Kim today. Following her and Danny with his eyes, he gives them both encouraging, affectionate tweets.

Eventually it can't be put off any longer, and we set off north to the Nesbitts'.

Danny hangs his head. 'I shouldn't be playing with Kim any more,' he mutters as we walk along. 'I'm only making it harder for her if she's going to end up a guard dog. I need to give her less attention. Yeah, that's best. You stay with her while I walk ahead, Jess.'

It doesn't work, of course. Danny keeps forgetting Kim's not supposed to be alongside him, and when he does remember, and strides off, Kim just treats it as a game, padding up to Danny to nuzzle his legs.

We make our way across fields towards the north-eastern part of town. Kim remains happy until Danny veers towards a group of high-rise flats. That's when the paw-dragging starts. As we near a concrete tower block surrounded by dead grass, rubbish and busted bikes, Kim tries to bolt.

'Just a bit further,' Danny soothes her, clutching her collar firmly. 'Good girl. You're the best.'

With her tongue lolling sideways, Kim – torn between wanting to obey Danny and running off – stumbles on.

We reach a black steel door splashed with graffiti.

As soon as she sees it, Kim collapses on the ground.

Danny closes his eyes a moment, then pulls her gently to her feet. 'We have to,' he murmurs. 'I'm sorry, Kim, I'm sorry.' His coaxing gets her shakily upright again. 'Good girl,' he whispers. 'You'll be fine. You'll be . . . ' His voice falls away.

I move closer to Danny. Twigs – eyes alert for danger – folds his wings in tight.

Danny keeps a firm hold of Kim's collar. Then he takes a deep breath and raps on the black door.

After a long wait, there's a heavy rattle of locks.

Hearing it, Kim utters a haunting whimper and Danny steps back, readying himself.

The door is pushed open, banging hard against a side wall.

A man steps out.

He's tough-looking. Very tough. Around thirty years old. Bald and heavily muscled, with a tattoo of a werewolf spread across his neck. The tattoo is scarlet and so bright that Twigs squawks in surprise. The man sees him, gives me a cool appraising stare, then turns to Danny. The brief smile he gives him doesn't reach his eyes.

'So there she is. The runaway.'

The man's voice is intimidating. Twigs, concerned about a threat to me, hisses at him.

'Are you Steve?' Danny asks.

142

The man gives Twigs a wary glance, then nods at Danny. 'Yeah. Should have known Kim would run back to you.' He yawns, stretching out his wide shoulders. 'Don't give me that offended look, kid. We haven't done anything nasty to her, whatever you might think. She's just easily frightened.'

'I know she is,' Danny says, keeping his stare level. 'She's . . . she's not meant to be a guard dog.'

Steve looks annoyed by the comment. It's obvious he's not used to kids standing up to him. 'She's not happy with the training, that's for sure,' he grunts. 'She's a dozy thing. My daughter would do a better job of protecting our house right now.'

Danny forces out a laugh. 'Yeah, you're right. You must be able to tell by now that Kim won't be any use to you.'

'She'd better be,' Steve mutters. 'I paid good money for her.'

Danny nods. 'Sorry about that,' he says, 'but she's not the only dog around here. What if I can find you another one that's better for guarding?'

Steve snorts. 'And you'll convince the Fletchers to return my money, I suppose?'

'I'll try,' Danny says, and I can't believe how steady his voice is. 'Will you give Kim back to the Fletchers if I can convince them to return your money and I find you another dog?'

Steve Nesbitt pauses to look at Danny in a new way.

'The Fletchers need that money, kid. How are you going to persuade them? Walk all their other dogs for a year?'

'If I have to,' Danny says.

At that, Steve Nesbitt brays out a laugh. 'You look like you would, too.' He shakes his head. 'You've got some guts, coming round here asking for my dog, I'll give you that.' He hesitates, then raises his square chin. 'All right. I can't believe I'm doing this, but, tell you what – return my cash, and you can have Kim. As long as I get a full refund, that is. I want my money back. Every penny of it.'

As Danny nods, Steve steps forward and there's a brief shake of hands. Then, with a tenderness I'm not expecting, Steve bends towards Kim and takes her head in his rough palms. He ruffles her ears. Then he says to Danny, 'You really love this dog, don't you?'

Danny swallows.

'Yeah, thought so,' Steve says. 'Two lovers if ever I saw them. Romeo and bloomin' Juliet. After you called round here yesterday, Kim cried for hours at the sound of your voice. I've never seen a dog do that before.' The chuckle he gives is so deep that it sounds like a growl. 'OK, we have a deal,' he says. 'I'll trust you about the money, and I'll ring the Fletchers. You might as well take Kim back to your own house now if she's leaving anyway. No point having her here moaning all night, now she's seen you. She'll only keep us awake.'

'I can't take her to mine,' Danny says, his face falling. 'Mum won't . . . not in the house . . .'

'Oh, yeah. Forgot,' Steve says. 'Not too keen, is she? You'd better take Kim back to the Fletchers then, I suppose.'

'Yeah, I'll do that.'

Danny is about to lead Kim away when I say to him, 'Er, if the Fletchers don't mind, why don't you stay at my house tonight?'

'With Kim, you mean?' Danny stares wide-eyed at me. 'Is there enough room?'

'We'll make room.'

'You're serious? Your dad will be OK with that?'

'I don't know,' I admit. 'But I'll ask him.'

When I do, Dad says, 'As long as we can get permission from Danny's mum.'

Danny seems nervous when he rings her, but she agrees he can stay 'for one night only' as long as Kim goes straight back to the Fletchers in the morning. When the call ends I can't believe how happy Danny is.

We eat at my house. Dad buys some dog food at the local shop for Kim – which she wolfs down – and afterwards we head upstairs and squeeze everyone into my room.

Is Twigs jealous of Kim being in his territory? If so, he doesn't show it. He just plays his usual games, with Kim looking on in shy curiosity.

Dad comes up after a while to make sure we've got everything we need and to set up a camp mattress for Danny.

'What games do you like playing with Twigs, Mr Soper?' Danny asks him.

Dad shrugs awkwardly. 'I haven't got a favourite. I'm not as good at playing with Twigs as Jess. Anyway, who's playing with whom here? I have to wonder sometimes.'

'What do you mean?' Danny says, curling his hands in Kim's fur.

'I mean that Twigs will do anything for Jess, that's what.' Dad gives me a sideways grin. 'Twigs doesn't realise who the pet is around here. He thinks he's playing games that Jess likes, looking after *her*. Now that her gran's gone he's decided he's got to take care of her, and he's doing it every way he can. It's pure love.' Dad strokes Twigs' legs. 'You'd let Jess lead you anywhere, wouldn't you, Twigsy? You'd walk off the edge of the world for her.'

After Dad goes back downstairs, a text message comes through from the Fletchers on Danny's phone. He shows it to me. They've agreed he can keep Kim with him tonight, but they're not happy about giving Steve Nesbitt his money back.

You'd better have a convincing explanation tomorrow, the text reads. *We didn't sell her just so you could bring her back.*

I chew my lip, thinking Danny is in big trouble, but he's smiling. 'They aren't saying no, are they?' he says. 'All I've got to do is show them I'll do anything to make it up to them.'

'But how will you do that?'

He shrugs. 'Mow their lawn, wash their car, paint their house. Anything they want. Who cares?' He laughs and, seeing his face, so do I.

Twigs lets us know it's getting late by dragging the door open with his beak and waddling towards the bathroom. Kim and Danny follow us there, and we do our usual splash and tooth-clean.

'GIVE UZ A KISS,' Twigs says to Kim, but his mouth is so full of water it comes out more like 'GITH UTH A KITH.'

Kim wags her tail and licks the wet sink.

A few minutes later we're back in the bedroom doing the hairdryer trick. Twigs – wings fully outstretched – loves every single second, and so, when we turn the dryer on her, does Kim. She won't stop barking and running around. It's obvious how much she's enjoying herself. I can hardly believe this is the same dog I saw cowering outside the Nesbitt house just a few hours ago. She's completely chilled out now she's back with Danny.

Twigs leads Kim up to the window. He shows her the garden and the birds. Its dark out there, and Kim, of course, hasn't a clue what Twigs is getting all excited about.

Later, there's no restless scrambling before Twigs settles down for the night. When it's time to go to sleep he just wants me to put the green blanket over my bed so he can lie next to me. Danny plonks down on the camp mattress, with Kim curled in a huge ball at his feet.

Before I switch off the beside lamp I pick up Lucy's pink Fluffy poem pad. There are still five more poems I haven't read. Even though we've done the poetry with the Year Twos at school, it feels like a duty now to finish them.

'Yeah, go on then,' Danny says when I suggest reading them out. 'Let's hear them.'

I recite four, then check with Twigs and Danny. 'Want the final one?'

Twigs doesn't look enthusiastic, but he doesn't object either. Danny nods. Kim shuffles up and licks his nose.

'It's called "Stroky Ears",' I tell them, and I try to read it with true feeling, like Lucy did to the Year Twos:

'More beautiful than a dove,
Fed on lettuce and love,
You have irresistibly stroky ears,
And I've loved you for years and years and years.'

Twigs shakes his head. 'Nutter,' he murmurs. Then, 'Night night.'

'Night night, Twigs,' Danny says, turning onto his side and circling his arm around Kim. Well, halfway round. He can't reach all the way over her back.

Kim is restless when I first turn off the light, but she soon settles down when Danny falls asleep.

Twigs stays close beside me. I watch his eyes gradually close as he leans his heavy weight against my shoulders, the feathers of his tail tickling my arm. 'Head in the bed?' I whisper. It's a little game we play sometimes, where Twigs hides his head under the blankets and then shows it to me again.

Tonight he's too weary, though. He just gazes at me as I swish the green blanket across us.

'Sweet dreams,' I murmur and, when I peek across at him less than a minute later, he's fast asleep.

Fourteen

The next morning is Saturday, the day of the school festival, and we're all under strict instructions from Mrs Baldwin to be there by nine o'clock to help her set up the class stall.

After an early breakfast at our house, Danny is picked up by his mum. It's obvious how anxious she is to get Kim into her car and back to the Fletchers'. Lifting Kim into the rear seat, Danny stops for a second to give me a resigned shrug.

I ruffle Kim's ears through the open back window and smile at Danny. 'Good luck persuading them to give Steve Nesbitt his money back,' I say, touching his arm.

'Yeah, thanks,' he mutters, with a determined smile.

*

Dad drops me off with Twigs at the school fifteen minutes later. 'I'll be back soon,' he tells me. 'Just got to pick someone up first. I'll bring him along later. You're going to like him.'

I've no idea what Dad means by that, and he won't tell me more, so I head towards our class stall.

Mrs Baldwin has 6B's best work proudly on display, with our stall lined up alongside the others on the football pitch. Since I haven't been at Ashcroft High long, I don't have much to show, except my artwork, including one or two drawings I've done for a project on insects that the twins have been working on all year. Mrs Baldwin apparently always has a theme, and this time that theme is 'THE NATURAL WORLD' so there's also a History of Dogs by Danny prominently displayed, plus the work the whole class have done this week on cockatoos and other endangered birds.

Oh, and Lucy's poems, of course. They're pasted everywhere.

Parents and other visitors start arriving just after ten o'clock. Every stall draws attention, but our stall gets the most. Why? Twigs, of course! He's shrieking and squonking non-stop. Plus the twins are pretty good at gathering people in.

'Come and see Twigs the Nutter!' Angus is yelling. 'And Hairy Jim, our hamster! Put your fingers in the mystery box. Feel how cute he is!'

151

'And while you're at it,' Hamish adds when Mrs Baldwin gives him a glare, 'check out the latest poetry by Lucy Daniels. She's improvising poems today on any subject you want. So far we've had plates, motorways, chimneys, toilets and other great things like that. How does she do it? Look!' he calls out as Lucy, scribbling furiously, hands him a new sheet of paper. 'She's just written another one. Amazing! It's called . . .'

'"Pavement Cracks",' Lucy whispers.

A balding, elderly man leans over to study the poem. He's already rifled through several. After carefully reading 'Pavement Cracks', he levels his gaze at Lucy.

'Do you have any more verses along these lines?'

Lucy is so astonished to be asked about her poetry by anyone except us or Mrs Baldwin that she can't answer him.

The elderly man waits patiently, his eyes crinkling into a smile.

'Yes, she has,' I jump in when Lucy stays frozen. 'There are loads of others . . .'

'Here,' Mrs Baldwin says proudly, handing him a folder.

The man reads all the poems inside the folder – and I mean *all* of them. 'Interesting,' he says to Lucy at last. 'I take it that many of your other poems are at home?'

She nods tightly.

'I thought so,' he mutters. 'There's real originality here, and I'm intrigued by your unusual choice of subjects. I think your verses might be exactly the prod my undergraduate students need to chivvy them along.' He smiles at Lucy. 'I wonder if I might possibly borrow "Pavement Cracks" and a few others from you? I would send them back to you via the school, of course. I'd like to show them to a few people.'

'Show them?' Lucy squeaks.

'Yes,' the man says.

Mrs Baldwin takes the man aside and they agree that Lucy will select some of her favourites and post them to his address.

The man smiles again at Lucy. 'Do, indeed, send me as many as you wish. And, if it's not too much trouble, may I take "Pavement Cracks" with me today? I'd really like to read it aloud to a colleague.'

Lucy manages to blink and nod.

'Thank you.' The man opens his wallet and hands Mrs Baldwin a business card. Then he turns back to Lucy. 'My name is Alexander Holme, by the way. I'm a Professor of English and Poetry at King's College, London.'

And with that he heads off, tightly clasping 'Pavement Cracks'.

The beautiful transformation that comes over Lucy's face can't be described. She doesn't – can't – move until he's completely gone.

'Did . . . did . . . did . . .' She gets stuck on that for a while. 'Did . . . did you see . . .'

'Yeah, we saw, Luce, we saw,' Angus laughs. 'Judging from the way his eyes were popping out of his head, you should have asked for some money for that poem, though.'

'Oh, Luce,' I say, hugging her. 'The look on his face! And a professor of poetry, too . . .'

Mrs Baldwin takes Lucy's arm. 'The first poetry professional to show an interest in your work,' she whispers to her, 'but it won't be the last.'

While Lucy stays in a daze I keep an eye on Twigs. Cooped up in his transportation cage, he's irritable, but he's entertaining the crowds nicely. People gasp over him all morning, though he does keep spitting at the noisy ones. To distract him I occasionally lob pine nuts his way.

I'm concerned when, an hour later, there's still no word from Danny about the Fletchers, but I'm so busy with Twigs that I haven't got much time to think about it.

'Who's that man who keeps looking over here?' Hamish asks me a bit later.

The mystery man he's talking about arrived with Dad around half an hour ago, and Dad takes his time before he brings him over. Asking Mrs Baldwin if he can borrow me for a moment, Dad takes me to a spot a few feet away where we can have some privacy.

'I'm not deliberately springing another surprise on you,' he tells me out of earshot of everyone else. 'I just thought that since Twigs is already here it would be easier. Will you meet someone?'

I'm not sure what I'm getting into, but I nod and Dad brings the stranger to the stall.

'Hello,' the man says, 'you must be Jess.' He's stocky, grey-bearded, and has a soft London accent. 'I'm Alfie Parks, a retired police officer,' he tells me. 'Your dad found me on the *Birdfinder* website. I've got quite a bit of Moluccan experience, and I'm hoping to help you out with Twigs on weekdays. Your dad thought this might be a good chance for us to say hello. It's great to meet a fellow Moluccan devotee.'

He holds out his hand to shake, and I take it.

'Hi,' I say guardedly.

I already know who he is, of course. Alfie Parks is the man Dad has mentioned several times already. When I did finally check his advert online it scared me because Dad's right: Alfie Parks *does* have a lot of experience handling Moluccans. He lives nearby, too. But I've put off talking to Dad about him. I'm still not ready to trust anyone else to look after Twigs yet. Especially a stranger.

I try smiling, but as I look at Alfie stabs of fear are jumping right though me.

155

'And this' – he stares up at the transportation cage – 'must be the one and only Twigsy-Twiglet!'

Alfie laughs when Twigs lunges at him through the bars.

'Ha! I don't blame you, fella. I'm a scary-looking geezer, right enough!' He turns back to me. 'I've heard Twigs' full story from your dad, Jess. Your gran came along at just the right time in his life, by the sound of things. And you've been fighting his cause ever since. Lucky Twigs, I'd say.'

'Thank you,' I mutter warily.

'You've done amazingly well to keep Twigs this happy,' he says. 'Your dad tells me that Twigs recently had to move from a home he'd been in for years. Most older Moluccans would be a bundle of nerves by now if that happened. You're obviously an exceptional bird handler.'

As I shrug, Alfie gives me a shrewd glance. 'No one's told you that before, have they? Of course the average person knows nothing about how much skill and dedication is required to take care of a bird with a Moluccan's intelligence.'

I take a long breath. I wasn't expecting Alfie to be like this. I look for faults in him, but it's hard to find any.

Fortunately, a diversion turns up.

Mr Ginty.

I'm not surprised he's come over. The twins

photocopied my sketch of him running away from Twigs and they've been quietly selling it to his own form, 8C, all day. Mr Ginty's been nosing around all the stalls, trying to figure out who's distributing it.

Mrs Baldwin has pretended not to notice.

'Always a pleasure to see you, sir,' Angus says. 'Perhaps you'd like to put your hand in this box and feel how warm and cuddly our hamster is?'

Mr Ginty frowns at him, smoothing back his hair. His teeth sink into a cone of chocolate ice cream bought at the central refreshment tent.

'I see the squawker is back,' he mutters, giving Twigs a filthy look.

Mrs Baldwin's smile is like a beam of light. 'Yes, we brought him in just for you, Harold.'

Mr Ginty grunts, picking up a sheaf of Lucy's poems. He reads one briefly, then makes a point of rolling his eyes. At the same time, his ice cream cone dangles close to Twigs' cage.

Twigs doesn't need an invitation. There's a little bar that holds the door of his transportation cage closed. I had no idea he'd worked out how to open it, but that's what he does now. It springs wide, and with a screeched *'Dong-ding-dong!'* Twigs hops out, snatches Mr Ginty's ice cream cone in his beak, leaps to the ground and runs off with it.

'What? Wha—' Mr Ginty stumbles after him across the field. 'Give me that! *Give it back!*' he shouts, only stopping when he sees people laughing at him.

Enjoying the chase, Twigs returns to wiggle the ice cream provocatively at Mr Ginty. 'WHOA!' he taunts. 'NUTTER! GIVE UZ A KISS!'

Mr Ginty's face reddens, which brings another huge roar of laughter from people nearby. Trying to remain dignified, Mr Ginty lifts his nose and strides back to 8C's stall.

But Twigs isn't finished yet. He races after Mr Ginty, zigzagging across the grass. Mr Ginty pretends he's not concerned at first but, when Twigs closes in, he starts trotting to get away. The faster Mr Ginty goes, the quicker Twigs chases him until, with a little squeal, Mr Ginty slips, falling over on a wet patch at the edge of the field. His trousers get covered in mud.

Mrs Baldwin steps up behind me. 'Well, well, what a pity,' she says, smiling away.

'GALA-GALA-GEENY!' Twigs hops up to a chair beside one of Mr Ginty's students. Transferring the ice cream cone from his beak to a claw, he daintily hands it to him.

Mr Ginty is so shocked at looking foolish that he pretends he's heading for his car. 'You students on my stall . . . I'll be back shortly,' he manages. 'I've just received an important phone call . . . It's very, very important.'

As Mr Ginty opens his car door and slides onto the seat, his muddy backside smears dirt all over the

158

gleaming blue leather upholstery. Looking furious, he clenches his teeth and drives away.

As soon as Mr Ginty is out of earshot the whoops and cheers that go up from 8C's stall can be heard all over the field.

'Brilliant!' Angus shouts. 'That was *so* brilliant!'

He's right, but I'm worried about getting Twigs back inside his cage – there could be all sorts of dangers out here. Luckily, Twigs runs straight back to our stall, jumping up onto one of the tables. It's only then I realise something – Twigs was so excited about chasing Mr Ginty that he's been running freely about *outside*.

I gasp, staring at him.

Twigs flicks his tail and does a stylish pirouette for us. 'WHOOO!' he screams. 'WHOO-WAAA! WHOO-WAAAA!'

'Twigs, you little genius!' Hamish punches the air.

'Did we really see that?' Angus asks as Twigs throws his head wildly from side to side. 'Please tell me someone caught it on camera!'

Rising up on her toes, Lucy strokes Twigs' neck. 'Twigsy-Twiglet!' she yells. 'Twigs the champion! Twigs the hero!'

'YEAH!' Twigs yells, and at the sound of it a huge shout and round of applause goes up from the students on 8C's stall, and I see Alfie Parks and Dad laughing and clapping, too.

Twigs loves hearing his own name, of course. Everything about him looks proud: his huge grey feet, his outspread wings, his fanned tail. 'WHOA! BONJOUR! WHOA!' he bellows, his crest hitching higher and higher as he builds up to a series of skull-blasting hoots.

'Here we go,' Dad groans, hands over his ears, but he looks proud, too, and Twigs, encouraged by all the clapping and cheering, goes completely berserk, letting off one piercing scream after another.

Eventually Mrs Baldwin glances worriedly at me. 'He won't carry on like this forever, will he, Jess?'

'He might,' I tell her.

After chasing Mr Ginty away, Twigs becomes so popular at the festival that we can hardly cope with all the visitors to our stall.

Danny finally turns up about an hour later. His mum is with him, but they're not walking together. Danny strides ahead. His mum says something to him, but he ignores whatever it is, leaving her behind. When he reaches our stall, we all crowd around him. Danny can't even raise his face.

'What happened?' Hamish asks.

'The Fletchers told you no, didn't they?' I say.

'They tell me they need the money,' he murmurs at last. 'Kim's got to go back to the Nesbitts. I said I'd do whatever they want – jobs, chores, anything, *anything* – but they need the cash now.'

As Danny gives us the details of his conversation with them his mum stays away, occasionally glancing guiltily at him from the other stalls. Mrs Baldwin finds something for Danny to do, and we all keep close to him.

It stays busy, and the crowds press around Twigs. They only break up when it starts to rain. The downpour is heavy and, while we pull a cover over the little roof of our stall, most people rush for shelter inside the big central refreshment tent.

I use the distraction to calm Twigs down. He isn't happy about the wet weather. He might not be frightened of being outdoors any more, but he still doesn't like rain, and he squawks in complaint until I get his cage under cover.

It's nearly an hour later, just as the rainstorm is ending, that Kim arrives.

'Jess . . .' Lucy brings her hands to her lips.

We can all see why Lucy is so shocked. Kim is soaked – so cold and sopping wet that she can barely stand. Nobody can believe the exhausted state she's in as she struggles across the grass.

'She must have been walking through the storm since it began,' Lucy whispers.

'Oh, Kim . . .' I murmur.

She gives a defeated, hopeless bark. Then she coughs, staring around blearily. It's obvious who she's looking for.

The twins appear at my shoulder.

'Come on,' I say, and we all head towards her.

But the first to reach her is Danny. His mum is close to him, and for a second it looks like she's trying to hold him back. Maybe she is, maybe she isn't, but nothing is going to do that. Danny runs across the field and has Kim in his arms in seconds.

Lucy and I hurry off to find towels. When we get back, Danny uses them to clean Kim's muzzle. It's caked in mud.

'Let me help,' I say, removing my jacket.

With his mum looking on in silence, Danny dries Kim's shaking legs. All she wants to do is get close to him. Shivering uncontrollably, pressing against Danny, she scrunches up against his hip as if he's the only bit of warmth left in the world.

'What made Kim come so far in this storm?' Lucy asks me. I shake my head, but I can guess – she's just decided that she's always going to run back to Danny now, if she can, even if that means escaping from the Fletchers.

Danny's mum moves away across the field. Taking out her mobile phone, she starts speaking to someone.

We all finish drying Kim. Cradled in Danny's

arms, she looks exhausted. She keeps peering around as well, as if she knows it's only a matter of time before someone's going to take her away from him again.

Twigs, safely back in his cage, peers solemnly at me, then at Kim.

Finally, after a long conversation on the phone, Danny's mum heads back towards us.

'Are you OK?' she asks Danny.

He doesn't answer or look at her. Instead, his hands stay clutched tightly around Kim. 'What's happening?' he finally mutters. 'Is Jimmy Fletcher coming to pick her up?'

'No, he's not,' she says.

'Why not?' Danny suddenly looks scared. 'Jimmy's not giving her back to the Nesbitts right now, is he? Mum, he can't—'

'No, he's not doing that,' his mum interrupts.

Danny can't keep the anxiety out of his voice. 'Mum, what do you mean? What's going on? How come the Fletchers aren't taking her back?'

She folds her arms. 'They're not taking her back because I've told them we're going to buy her.'

A dumbfounded look spreads across Danny's face. 'What?' he gasps. 'But you said . . . you told me . . .' He stands up, and Kim stands with him. 'You said we can't afford it. You said—'

'I know what I said.' His mum reaches out to him, holding his face in her hands. 'I've said a lot of things in my life. I've changed my mind about a lot of things, too. Come on. We'd better find a lead for her.'

'A lead?' Danny's still standing there, open-mouthed.

'Yes, you know, one of those long ropey things.' Gripping his shoulders, she abruptly laughs and kisses him.

'A lead?' Danny splutters. 'So we can . . .'

'Yes,' she says. 'So we can take her home.'

Fifteen

The next week speeds past. Kim settles in with Danny and every day at school he's in a kind of stunned, happy trance, constantly talking about her. He can't quite believe she's really his.

He, Kim and Lucy start spending more time at my house as well. I'm really pleased about that – and so is Twigs. He loves Kim, but as the days rush by I'm growing more and more nervous. Why? Because I've agreed with Dad that we'll visit Alfie Parks' house on Saturday, that's why.

The trouble is, it still feels too soon. I know Dad needs a break, and Alfie does seem really nice, but I'm scared I might lose Twigs. Even if he's only with Alfie while I'm at school, I'm scared about letting Twigs go.

By the time Saturday arrives, I've made sure the others in the class are going to be there to support me on the visit to Alfie's. As Dad picks them up in our estate car, he's got an air of confidence about him which for some reason only makes me more edgy.

It's nearly sunset when we pull up outside Alfie Parks' ground floor flat. The weather's chilly. It's a cold October evening, and the forecast is for an especially frosty night. Twigs flaps his wings, restless from the journey as we clamber out. He shivers.

'I hope you don't mind us all trooping over like this,' Dad apologises to Alfie when he answers the door.

'Not at all.' Alfie's pleasant cockney voice ushers us in. 'Anyone interested in Twigs' welfare should be here. Come in, please. Everyone's welcome.'

There's a smell of chilli con carne wafting in from the kitchen as we enter. The flat is roomy, with lots of space. Secretly, I'd been hoping it would be too small for Twigs.

Alfie smiles at me, but in my touchy mood I only find his friendliness irritating. Danny, Lucy and the twins sit on a large couch across the room.

'Let him straight out,' Alfie says, as I place Twigs' cage on the living room carpet.

'Er, maybe not the best idea,' Dad suggests.

'No, no, it's fine,' Alfie assures him.

166

As soon as Twigs' cage is open he charges across the carpet, runs protectively between me and Alfie and screeches three times in his face.

The amazing thing is what happens next.

Alfie kneels down, puts his nose right up to Twigs' beak, and screeches back. 'RRREEEEEEEEEEEEE EEEEEEEEEE!'

It stuns Twigs into complete silence.

'Why did you do that?' I gasp, completely shocked. 'You scared him!'

Alfie opens his hands placatingly. 'Actually, I didn't, Jess. In the wild it's standard for Moluccans to challenge anything entering their territory. I was just letting him know whose territory this is – mine. Look. He's OK.'

I'm surprised to see that Alfie's right. Twigs is staring cautiously at him, but it's a look more of respect than fear.

'Wow, he's an impressive Moluccan all right,' Alfie says. 'A truly handsome boy. Terrific crest!'

'NUTTER!' Twigs shrieks in Alfie's face, showering him with a blizzard of white powder.

Alfie coughs, but instead of being offended by the powder he's amused. 'Oh, that hasn't happened to me in a long, long time. Too long!'

'SHUT UP!' Twigs screams, and the grinning Alfie nearly falls over with chuckling.

'Shut up, eh? Great stuff! Who taught him that?'

'Er . . . I think I did,' Dad admits, and Alfie bellows with laughter.

I'm trying not to like Alfie. 'You shouldn't be so loud around him,' I growl. 'Twigs is very sensitive.'

'Is he now? Sensitive, eh? Watch this.'

Alfie gives us all a wink and holds a pecan nut up to Twigs' beak. Twigs sees the nut, but as soon as he reaches up for it Alfie opens his hand – and the nut is gone.

Twigs hoots with frustration.

'That wasn't fair,' I protest.

'It's right here.' Alfie opens his other hand. The nut is inside. This time it's Lucy, Danny and the twins who laugh.

'Just a little trick,' Alfie says. 'Want to see how to make a bird your friend? Watch.'

Tossing the nut between his hands like a juggler, Alfie gets Twigs running in circles.

'You're just frustrating him!' I complain, even though I've played games like this with Twigs hundreds of times and know he loves them.

'That's not frustration I'm seeing.' Alfie whirls the nut around. 'Eagerness, more like. He wants to eat the nut, but he wants to play more. He's a bit stuck between the two things, and while all that's going on, hopefully he's forgetting that I'm a stranger, forgetting to be wary of me, and . . . here we go . . . look, I'll give him the nut . . .' which Alfie now does, quietly popping it into Twigs' beak, '. . . and I'll stroke him, *there, there* and *here*, and – what do you know? –Twigs and I are properly introduced!'

I stare in amazement. Apart from seeing him briefly at the school festival, Twigs has known Alfie all of five minutes and already he's perched on his arm, noisily chewing a pecan!

'I've got a garden, too,' Alfie tells us proudly as Twigs sniffs his face. 'He'll like that. You've done a great job with him, Jess. He's in superb condition for his age. Do you know how I can tell?'

'No,' I say numbly.

'His eyes are clear as a bell.'

Alfie spreads Twigs' wings. Astonishingly, Twigs simply allows him. He permits Alfie to expose even his inner feathers. Then Alfie rubs the very edges of his wingtips with tiny finger-strokes. I've never seen anyone handle a bird quite that way before. I had no idea how much Twigs might like it.

'How come he's not more wary of you?' Hamish marvels.

'Twenty-five years' experience of handling my own Moluccan,' Alfie says. 'My screams told Twigs I was his equal, but not a threat. After that, I'd have to give Twigs a new reason to fear me, and a little gentle holding is not going to do that. Did you know that unhappy Moluccans often end up plucking their own feathers out? There's not one missing on Twigs.

169

That's a real tribute to you, Jess.' Alfie breaks into a smile. 'I was around the same age as you when I got my first Moluccan. Baffy, she was called. Best bird I ever knew.'

'What happened to her?' Lucy asks.

Alfie sighs. 'She caught a disease when she was still fairly young. Broke my heart when she died, it did. I loved that girl. She was a noisy so-and-so, but aren't they all?'

'SHUT UP!' Twigs squawks – and nuzzles Alfie's arm.

Nuzzles him.

I can't believe it.

Dad blinks at Twigs, stupefied. The others look equally astonished.

'Cuppa tea, anyone?' Alfie casually picks Twigs up and carries him under his arm into the kitchen as if he's a lap dog used to being carted around.

I expect Twigs to peck his hand off, but he doesn't.

I expect Twigs to scream and squirm to get out of Alfie's hands, but he doesn't.

I expect – no, I realise, I *want* – Twigs to complain, but he doesn't.

My head's reeling. What's going on? I thought Gran and I were the only ones who could handle Twigs like this. I try to come up with an objection to Alfie, but my mind is blank.

Dad catches my eye. 'Isn't he special?' he mouths.

'Moluccans love play,' Alfie remarks, as I mechanically follow him into his kitchen. 'Hardly anyone can really be bothered to play properly with a bird, but I'm a bit of a kid myself. I love all that stuff.' He finishes making the tea and hands me a cup. 'There you go. Nice cuppa. Lovely jubbly. Are there any special tricks Twigs likes doing, Jess?'

Sitting at the counter, I find myself going through the motions of showing Alfie the games Twigs enjoys most.

Alfie watches closely and copies what I do. He plays the games well. Except for copycat, he plays them almost as well as me.

It all feels horribly wrong, and at first I've no idea why.

Then I know.

It's because these are *our* tricks – mine and Twigs'. Private. Between us. Between *us*. Even though I know it's stupid, I feel like I'm losing him already.

I retreat in a daze to the couch in the living room.

'He's good with Twigs, isn't he?' Lucy whispers, trying to reassure me. And it's true: Alfie is good, he's great, but right now that's the last thing I want to hear.

'We took Twigs to a zoo recently,' Danny tells Alfie. 'He saw other Moluccans for the first time. Do you know anyone else who's got a Moluccan? It would be brilliant if you did. It would remind Twigs he's not alone.'

171

Alfie gazes at me, and I know I should be saying something. I should be asking for his help as well. But for some reason I can't talk. I can't even meet his eye. Twigs isn't meant to give his heart to someone else! Who is this man already taking him away from me?

I feel a crushing jab inside me and know it's pure jealousy – but I can't help it. I realise what I want right now is for Alfie to mess up, to be useless. But I have to put Twigs first. He seems to like this man.

Swallowing my emotion, I meet Alfie's gaze. 'Danny's right. Twigs loved meeting those birds at Gurney Zoo. Can you help us? There has to be a way for him to see Moluccans again.'

'Tricky, tricky.' Alfie rubs his beard. 'Finding Moluccans these days is a tall order. They're so rare now. There's not much hope of finding any in this area, but I'll try. Let me look into it.'

Dad obviously loves Alfie, and I can understand why. He's the answer to Dad's prayers.

So why am I feeling so bad? Why am I churning inside? It's not as if Alfie isn't nice. He is, and he's making it easy for me to let Twigs go to him. But that only makes my heart sink because . . . because Twigs is my last link to Gran, and somehow it feels like I'm letting go of her as well.

I close my eyes, then open them again. Until now, Twigs has been happily pottering about with Alfie.

But as soon as he sees the lost expression on my face he jumps up beside me on the couch. Rubbing my hands with his beak, he says, 'JESS . . . JESS?'

Dad, stirring a cup of tea, doesn't hear. 'Twigs seems to like you a lot,' he tells Alfie.

'Oh, nonsense,' Alfie tuts, watching me closely. 'Don't mistake the way Twigs has accepted me today for real affection. I'm just a good bird handler, that's all. The way Twigs mirrors Jess, always finding where she is, checking on her . . . well, I've never seen anything like it before. It's remarkable. It'll take me years to develop a bond like that. I'll probably never do so.' He stares right at me. 'I can see how much you both love each other.'

More cups of tea are passed round. What is it with all these cups of tea? While sugar is being spooned out, I gaze at the carpet. Why does Alfie have to be so nice? I don't want his sympathy. I don't want his praise. Right now I just want to be on my own with Twigs, a long way from here.

Twigs gives me a cautious *'what's the matter?'* hoot.

I can't look at Alfie any more.

Seeing that, Lucy gently squeezes my arm. Danny gets up. The twins stand up, too, and hover close. No one is drinking their tea. They're all just looking at me. I try to hide what I'm feeling but I can't.

'You've done a fantastic job of looking after Twigs, Jess,' Alfie says quietly. 'You should be proud. And,

173

remember, I'm only helping your dad out here. Evenings and weekends will be all yours.'

I don't know what to say. I should be grateful, but I'm empty. I can tell Alfie will be good to Twigs, but the *closeness* . . . I can't bear the closeness. *I'm* the one Twigs is supposed to be close to.

'Has Twigs ever bitten you?'

I realise Alfie's asking a question.

'Never,' I murmur.

He nods. 'Baffy was the same. They don't bite the ones they love. I bet Twigs has his own way of kissing you as well.'

'Yes,' I say woodenly.

'How does he do it?'

I almost don't answer. 'He licks my cheek.'

Alfie pats his hairy chin. 'Baffy used to rub her lower beak right here. Every Moluccan does it in their own way.' He smiles at me. 'It'll always be between you and Twigs, Jess – that special affection, I mean. I'm not intending to take him away from you. I'm just borrowing him for a while. If you'll let me, that is. If you'll do me the honour.'

I can feel tears forming in my eyes. I'm not even trying to hide them any more. They're selfish tears. They're somehow tears for my gran as well. An image comes into my mind of her, and I suddenly wish with all my heart that she was here right now to stand up for me and say something.

174

When Dad pops out to use the toilet, I can't contain myself any more. 'I don't want you to take him, Alfie,' I rasp. 'Can you say no to Dad? Can you say you've changed your mind? Please. Make an excuse. Please. I'll do anything. *Please.*'

'You won't lose him,' Alfie tells me. 'Jess, I'll only—'

He breaks off as Dad returns, and an awkward silence falls over the room. 'I see that you've kept Twigs' flight feathers intact,' Alfie remarks to fill the gap. 'You've let them grow to full length.'

The comment is true enough, but it irritates me.

'Gran cut them, but I haven't bothered,' I snap.

'You should,' Alfie says mildly. 'If you don't, he'll fly off eventually.'

I'm spoiling for a fight – and suddenly here's my chance.

'He won't *fly off*,' I growl. 'He's never *flown off*. He won't leave me. Don't you understand? He won't leave me – ever. *Ever.* Look, I'll show you.'

I'm almost shouting now. I don't know what's wrong with me. I'm just desperate to prove Alfie wrong about something. Anything.

Without thinking, I pick Twigs up and stride towards the front door. There's a large garden beyond it.

Marching out about ten feet, I place Twigs on the lush grass. There are trees all around us and, beyond the trees, neighbouring houses.

175

From the second I put him down, Twigs is alarmed about being outside. Yes, he ran after Mr Ginty at the school festival, but that was daytime. Now it's almost dark and he's frightened.

I deliberately stand in the middle of the lawn to prove my point.

With a gusty wind tugging at his feathers, Twigs begins hobbling back towards the house. He stops when he sees I haven't moved.

'JESS!' he calls, wanting me safely back inside.

'See!' I yell at Dad and Alfie. They're standing together on the front porch with the others. 'See! I told you! Twigs won't go in if I'm out here! He won't leave me.'

'JESS! JESS!'

Twigs tips his face to one side, hooting woefully. It starts raining. Only a few drips, but they scare him. Twigs desperately wants to get out of it, but flutters back for me instead. He thinks the rain is injuring me. Letting out one distressed peal of anguish after another, he grabs the hem of my jeans in his beak, trying to haul me in.

'JESS! JESS! *JESSSSSSS!*'

I can feel his heart thudding against my shin, and suddenly I realise that what I'm doing is crazy. I've got to get him inside.

'Sorry, sorry,' I whisper tearfully, and Twigs lets out a relieved cry as we head towards Alfie's front door.

That's when Lucy screams.

'Behind you!' Danny shouts, and the twins race down the garden.

Whirling around, I see it – a ginger cat.

It's a big one. Half-hidden until now in the tall grass, its olive-green eyes are tracking Twigs with absolute focus.

Twigs hasn't seen it. He's still too busy worrying about me. He's screeching at the top of his lungs to hurry me in.

Hamish, dashing down the garden, leaps in front of the cat – but too late.

It pounces on Twigs unbelievably fast, its claws raking his legs and slashing at his neck. Only Twigs' sheer size keeps him upright.

Before I can rescue Twigs, the cat's teeth sink into his chest and suddenly there's a tearing noise – a *ripping*.

Twigs is so shocked that he doesn't make a sound.

Danny finally gets a firm hand on the cat's rear end and drags it off.

We all turn to Twigs.

He spins . . . and topples to the ground.

He staggers.

From the puzzled look in his eyes, it's obvious he has no idea what's happened. He only knows he's hurt.

'Twigs,' I sob, reaching for him.

The cat squirms from Danny's grip and has a second

lunge at Twigs, but this time I'm in front of it. I get a slash of claws across my fingers, but distract it long enough for the twins and Alfie to smother the cat in a jacket and carry it away.

As I kneel in front of Twigs, he totters in a confused hop-step.

Then he looks at his chest.

For a second that's all he does – stares down at the red triangle blooming across his feathers. Blood. So much blood.

He gazes in a terrified way at me then – for reassurance – and gives a smudgy cough of panic.

'Twigs,' I whisper, my eyes blurring with tears. I reach for him again, but Twigs retreats. He's in shock. He turns a few times in tight circles, as if he's still trying to find the cat.

'It's OK,' I murmur. 'Twigs . . .'

And it's then, as I'm whispering his name, trying to grasp him, that Twigs does the last thing I expect.

He opens his wings. He fans them solidly. And then, thrusting off with his claws, he leaps.

Skyward.

Sixteen

Twigs is in the air.

It's clumsy, but he's flying.

FLYING!

No, I think. *Not now. You're wounded. Any other time. But not now.*

Stuttery wingbeats take him to the top of a nearby fence pole.

'Twigs, come back!' I yell, but the words emerge as a whisper. His chest feathers are stained scarlet with blood, but as he rises I can see that Twigs isn't thinking about that. Flight. Real flight. Raw flight. He's a bird. He's in the sky, and nothing's going to stop him.

His huge creamy body lurches . . . and he soars upward again.

He veers crazily at first, then slowly gains height.

No. No. No.

Lucy's hands rise to her cheeks. 'Where's he heading, Jess?'

I stifle a sob. 'I don't know!'

Danny reaches my shoulder. 'Twigs! Come back! Twigs!'

Alfie steps forward. 'He's scared, reacting on pure instinct. He'll seek out safety. He's a bird, so that means—'

'I know,' I whisper. 'He'll go to the highest point he can find. We've got to catch him before he gets lost. Come on!'

I clutch Lucy's hand and we all race together in the same direction as Twigs. His light plumage means he looks like a ghost – or some kind of huge blood-spattered owl – in the darkening sky. Wide flaps of his wings take him ever higher.

'He's heading to that tree!' Hamish shouts, and I nod as Twigs flaps towards an enormous long-branched oak in a nearby park. Moments later, with a terrified *Mwwaaaaa*, he crashes onto the oak's highest branch, seizing it in his claws.

The sun has now set, and the wind shivers across us.

Angus is running beside me. 'Can Twigs survive in this?'

'It's not the cold that'll kill him,' I answer, my breath

coming in gasps. 'It's the blood he's losing. We have to get him to a vet!'

Alfie Parks and Dad trail behind, but we don't wait for them.

'Twigs!' I shout over and over.

We reach the oak tree. Twigs, high above, screeches when he hears my voice. Soft crying noises come from him. 'Mmm-mm, mmmm . . . mmmm . . .' He shuffles to the edge of the branch, but won't leave it.

Panic got him up there, I realise, but now he's too scared to fly down.

I start climbing, but an out-of-breath Dad, arriving at the same time as Alfie, holds me back.

'Twigs is smart, Jess,' Lucy says, clutching my arm. 'He'll find his way to us!'

'Yes, he just needs to calm down first,' Danny says. 'Then he'll figure it out.'

Angus waves his arms. 'Twigs! Look! We're here! Don't be scared! Fly down to us!'

We're all shouting now and, encouraged by that, Twigs does a little downward hop. Not far. Just to the next branch.

'Good,' I say, my stomach clenching with relief when I see what he's doing. 'It's like your obstacle course at home. That's right. Small steps. One branch at a time.'

'Come on, you can do it!' Hamish calls as Twigs picks his way slowly towards us.

A third of the way down, a sudden gust of wind nearly knocks him off the branch, and I stifle a scream.

'Keep going!' Danny yells.

Twigs stops for a moment to fluff out his wings, desperately trying to keep warm. Then he sets off down the tree again.

Hop along the branch. Jump. Regain his balance. Peer down at the next branch. Hop again.

He makes good progress at first, but soon comes to a stop. I can't understand why until he turns his chest towards us. It's heaving. He's finding it hard to breathe. But there's something else. Now he's closer I can see it – *movement* on his breast, trickling where the cat tore into him. Which can only mean one thing.

He's still bleeding.

I shudder, overwhelmed with guilt.

All of this is my fault. How could I take Twigs outside like that? How could I expose him to the cat? I wasn't thinking of Twigs. Only of myself. I didn't even keep his wings clipped. I let them grow, thinking one day I'd allow him to fly. Well, now he *has* flown, and because I didn't find him a safe place to spread his wings he's all alone up in a tree, bleeding to death.

I lean against Dad, breathing hard. What would Gran think of me now? She didn't ask a single thing of me when she left us. She didn't ask me to take care of Twigs. But I think she at least expected me to keep him away from danger. If there was one promise to keep, it was that.

Covering his face with his wings, Twigs trembles. He's managed to stumble his way halfway down the tree, but now he looks exhausted. Tiny, broken noises leak from him. 'Mmmm . . . mm . . . mmm . . .'

Swaying, he suddenly leans backwards, letting out a terrifying squawk as another blast of wind smashes into him.

'Twigs!'

Dad tries to stop me, but this time I avoid his grasping hands – and climb. There are hardly any footholds in the bark of the tree, but I don't care.

'Jess, come back!' Dad shouts.

Ignoring him, I scramble onto a stubby branch three feet above me.

From there I swing up.

Realising they can't catch me, Dad, Alfie, the twins and Danny arrange themselves below me in case I lose my grip.

When I get to within ten feet of Twigs I hear his whimpers. He can't properly grip the branch any longer. He's making constant crying sounds, but he's so cold that they barely escape his throat.

'*JESS!*' he wheezes, seeing me, and my stomach twists with guilt because, even now, he's more frightened for me than himself.

I look up and, as I do, Twigs falls backwards from the branch.

He's so tired that he doesn't even raise his wings to break his fall.

He plummets.

'*No!*' I scream.

I reach out to catch him – but miss.

Wet crunches echo up as Twigs strikes two branches below me.

I daren't look to see what's happened. For a moment there's only silence and a soft final *thump* as Twigs' body hits something.

Then there's a grunt.

I gaze between my legs to see Lucy's hands clutched to her chest. The twins are staring down at Danny. He's on his back. Twigs is splayed across his stomach.

'Jess,' Danny breathes out the word, crying with relief. 'I caught him. He's here.'

Seventeen

'Shush, shush, we're nearly there.'

I'm on the back seat of Dad's car, rocking Twigs gently in my arms. We're driving as fast as we can to a specialist avian vet Gran always used for Twigs – Mr Henry Stevens. Only Dad is with me. The others all wanted to come as well, but it's so late that instead they're at Alfie's, waiting to be picked up by their parents.

Twigs is wrapped inside my coat. He's drenched in blood. I'm holding him close, and from between my fingers he occasionally pops his frozen face up. His beak is so cold.

'Hurry, Dad,' I whisper. 'We haven't got much time.'

I'm shaking so much that I can hardly hold Twigs still. He's barely breathing, and every second of the journey I expect him to die in my arms. His whole body is riddled with cuts from the cat's claws. But it's his chest that's the hardest thing to look at. The wound reaches so deep into him that I can't see where it ends.

'*Please, please, please, please,*' I whisper.

By the time we reach the vet even the small cries Twigs was making have stopped.

'Bring him in,' Mr Stevens says urgently from the surgery entrance.

Seeing him, I weep with relief. A tall, balding man with a stoop, Mr Stevens ushers us through to his surgical room.

As he examines Twigs' chest wound he winces, stepping back a moment. 'Oh . . . there's been a really huge amount of blood loss.'

He repositions Twigs and begins a more thorough head-to-tail study. Lifting one of Twigs' wings, he takes a blood sample. The needle he uses is horribly wide. I flinch as I watch it go in, but Twigs doesn't react in any way. It's as if he's already too far gone to feel pain. His eyes are shut.

'I have to operate right away,' Mr Stevens tells us gravely. 'Twigs needs an immediate blood transfusion. But I must warn you that there's only a slim chance of saving him. This much blood loss could kill even a young, healthy bird, let alone one of Twigs' age.'

'Go on, do it then!' I shout, clutching Dad's hand. 'What are you waiting for? Do the transfusion!'

'There's something I need to tell you first.' Mr Stevens hesitates. 'Twigs' chest is . . . well, it's been torn. I'll need to put him under general anaesthetic to repair it. Birds often die under anaesthetic. So, given the shock he's had, even if I can physically repair the injury, there's a good chance he won't survive the surgery.'

I try to take that in. I can't.

'Do you understand?' Mr Stevens asks.

Dad nods, but I'm shaking.

Mr Stevens takes my hand. 'I know he's your bird now, Jess. Your gran told me how much you care for him, which is why I'm telling you this. Do you understand what I'm saying?'

'You're saying that . . .' I close my eyes, nearly choke, '. . . that Twigs is probably going to die, no matter what you do.'

'That's right. But – and I'm sorry to have to mention this – there's also the cost of the operation to consider. My materials are expensive, and . . .'

I gasp at how much the operation is going to cost. I know Dad doesn't earn that much.

'It's all right, Jess.' Dad puts his hand on my shoulder and turns to Mr Stevens. 'Go ahead. Save him if you can.'

After that Mr Stevens wastes no time. He wheels

Twigs away. As his surgery door closes I hug Dad, and then we wait.

Nearly an hour passes. During that time I just walk up and down the corridor outside the surgery, my stomach twisting in agony. I keep telling myself how tough Twigs is. He survived being torn from his nest. He survived all those early years stuck in Harry Smith's cage. He'll survive this, too.

Finally Mr Stevens emerges, pulling yellow plastic gloves off his hands. He smells horribly of disinfectant.

Somehow I ask it.

'He's . . . he's dead, isn't he? Twigs is dead.'

Mr Stevens blows out a long breath. 'No. Amazingly, he got through the surgery.' He shakes his head. 'Tough old bird. Very tough.'

I run up to him and clutch his waist. Tears burst out of my eyes and run down my cheeks.

Mr Stevens smiles. 'It's a good start, Jess, but please don't get your hopes up too much. The next few hours will be critical. He may not pull through. However, for now he's awake, and I've stitched him up. Do you want to go in and see him?'

'Yes,' Dad and I whisper together.

I cry as we enter the surgical room.

Twigs is lying on his right side on a square table. Bloody tissues lie all around him. There's a huge bandage on his chest as well. It's so big it covers half his body. Dozens of black stitches criss-cross his legs.

As I rush up Twigs hears my voice and turns a single exhausted blue eye towards me.

'Jjjjj . . .' He can't get my name out. His claws make feeble scrabbling noises on the tissue paper under him as he tries to get up.

'No, stay still,' I murmur.

I cup his head in my hands. His chest . . . oh, his chest. The beautiful plumage is all gone. The bandage runs all the way up to his neck. I place my thumb lightly on Twigs' cheek for him to rub against, and he offers me a weak lick. He says something as well, but the words come out so mangled I can't understand them.

'I'm here,' I reassure him. 'We're both here.'

Dad hovers close to Twigs, but is careful not to touch him.

'I can keep him here at the surgery if you want,' Mr Stevens tells us. 'It's calm and quiet, or—'

'Home,' I say. 'We'll take him home.'

'Good.' Mr Stevens nods. 'I'm sure he'd prefer that. I can't promise anything, but you'll know he's improving if his appetite returns. If he's going to live, at some point he'll get up and eat something. What's his favourite food?'

I hesitate, thinking of the treats the twins brought into class. 'Papaya,' I say.

'Then leave some papaya close to him.'

189

*

With Dad driving carefully along the dark streets to avoid jarring Twigs, we head home. There's none of the usual fierce gleam in Twigs' eyes as I cradle him in my arms.

I carry him straight upstairs to my room and line his cage floor with soft padded tissues. As I lift him towards the cage he struggles.

'Jsssss . . .'

He brushes my bed sheets with a wing – he wants to stay with me.

Kissing him, I place him on the covers and lie down next to him. Dad pulls up a chair beside us and glances at the clock. I can't believe the time: half past ten. Danny, Lucy and the twins are all at home now, but I wish they weren't. I wish they were here with me. Messages keep arriving from them, though.

Good or bad, Lucy texts me, *tell me what happens.*

Good or bad, I reply, though my hand is trembling when I type it.

The twins send me pictures of Twigs, including one taken by a student from school showing him chasing Mr Ginty with the ice cream sticking out of his beak.

He's a hero no matter what happens, Angus texts.

'I'll be there tomorrow,' Danny phones to say. 'In the morning I have to see my uncle. He's not well. But I'll come over as soon as I'm back.' His voice hesitates. 'Twigs will pull through. He'll be all right, Jess.'

After the call I lie back beside Twigs on the blankets. I'm tired but I'm not going to fall asleep. I can't risk rolling on top of him. Anyway, if Twigs does die (*and he won't, he won't*), I'm not having him go quietly without me realising it. He has to know I'm with him to the end.

Thinking that sets a shudder running though me, and Dad pulls his chair closer.

All night we stay like that, Dad and I hardly talking because I don't want to disturb Twigs while he's sleeping. The hours pass, and Dad is so amazing. I didn't know he cared this much.

More texts from the twins, Lucy and Danny come in just before dawn. I text them back: *He's hanging on.*

'Mr Stevens mentioned that the first twelve hours are the most critical,' Dad says, pressing my hand as the first rays of dawn hit the room. 'Twigs has already survived eight.'

I squeeze him back. I also place a fresh papaya the twins gave me a few days ago at the edge of the mattress, where Twigs can smell it.

When I see Dad yawning I tell him to go to bed.

'It's all right,' I say. 'I'll tell you if anything changes. Thanks, Dad. Without you . . .' I can't finish, and he hugs me.

*

Soon after Dad leaves, Twigs goes unbelievably still. Not knowing what's wrong, I stand above him, terrified that he's dead. When I press my fingertips lightly to his body my skin tingles with fear. The sound his heart is making isn't normal. I'm taken straight back to my childhood memory when Gran placed my hand against Twigs' chest. That was a steady, healthy thud. This is a constant, racing *d-d-d-d-d-d-d-d-d-d*, so fast that all the beats are running together.

He's fighting for his life.

Choking back a sob, I spread Twigs' green blanket across his body and lay my hands gently over him.

Just before nine o'clock in the morning, he gives a low throaty whistle in his sleep. '*Grruuu*,' he moans – a sound I've never heard from him before. Not long after that the shaking begins, little shivers that jolt through Twigs' wings. I don't think he can hear me, but all the way through them I talk to him. I tell him lots of things, but mostly I tell him I'm sorry.

Danny and the twins are still held up, but Lucy arrives in a rush around eleven o'clock. She crosses to the bed. As she kneels down in front of Twigs I can see how shocked she is. She tries to stop herself from bursting into tears, but can't quite manage it. We sit with our heads bent together, and she whispers, 'If Twigs had a hand, I'd hold it.'

'Don't give up hope,' I tell her. 'He's tough. All his life Twigs has been a survivor.'

'I know, I know,' she says, nodding fiercely.

She's brought fresh blueberries, pears and brazil nuts. 'Just in case he wants them,' she murmurs, placing them on the edge of the bed.

Mr Stevens rings after that. He can't keep the surprise out of his voice when I tell him that Twigs is still alive. He asks me to describe his condition.

'What do you mean, his condition?' I say. I'm too tired to understand what he means.

'Tell me how his eyes look, Jess.'

'He's asleep. He looks asleep!'

'I understand that, but hasn't he woken at some point? What did his eyes look like then?'

'They were . . . they were a bit . . . I don't know.'

'Murky and dull?'

'Yes.'

Mr Stevens pauses. 'They should be alert and have a nice transparent ring around them. The nasal openings on his upper beak ought to be open and clear as well. Describe how they look to you right now, Jess.'

I check. 'They're sore round the edges.'

There's an even longer pause this time. 'He's suffered very severe injuries.'

I don't like the new tone creeping into Mr Stevens' voice.

'Twigs is going to be OK,' I say, my voice rising.

'Prepare yourself to let him go, Jess,' he tells me. 'He's an old bird. A very brave one, but old. A cockatoo of Twigs' age hasn't got many reserves of strength. You've looked after him well. It's OK to let him go.'

He says something else but I hang up on him. I can't listen to anything like that. A few minutes later I ring him back and apologise. Between my tears, I say, 'Is there anything important I need to know right now to look after him better?'

'You know that white powder healthy Moluccans shed all the time?' he says. 'Is there any?'

With Lucy's help, I look. We carefully rifle through Twigs' feathers, but can't find any powder.

'He's stopped shedding,' Mr Stevens says, and I can tell how bad that is from his voice.

I'm still getting over the shock of that when the twins arrive. Dad lets them in, piling extra chairs into my room for everyone.

I've never seen Hamish and Angus looking so serious. They've brought Twigs a present – a shiny new rattle. Twigs stirs briefly when Hamish shakes it but he doesn't wake.

'I know he can't use it yet,' Angus says apologetically. 'But we just thought . . . you know . . . when he's better . . .'

Hamish stares at Twigs for a long time. 'He's just staying quiet,' he says. 'Saving his energy, that's what he's doing. Resting. Recovering.'

I nod, and we all sit in silence listening to morning birdsong in the garden. I open the window so Twigs can hear it, too.

Finally – catching us by surprise – Twigs wakes.

He shuffles upright, and we all jump to our feet, our eyes wide with relief.

'Is he better?' Angus asks.

'He might be thirsty,' Hamish suggests.

Lucy nudges my arm. 'Look! He's trying to get off the bed . . .'

She's right. Twigs' chest bandage trails a little behind, caught between his feet, as he jerks upright. In fact, he's in such a hurry to get to the floor that I only just catch him in time as he drops from the mattress.

When I go to pick him up, Twigs shakes me off. He won't let me hold him. What's he up to? Whatever it is, he wants to do it alone. Making tiny cries of pain, refusing any help from me, he staggers a few steps on the carpet.

'Where's he going, Jess?' Lucy whispers.

'Twigs, stay still,' I tell him. 'Just rest. *Rest*. You don't need to go anywhere.'

He rattles his wings at me from the floor, and I hear the bandage tighten and stretch on his chest. He picks at it with his beak, then leaves it alone.

'Come back here,' I whisper as Twigs staggers a few more steps. Shaking his head at me, he wobbles, tries to open his wings. Makes a defeated *paaaa* noise.

Then he starts pacing even faster around the bedroom carpet. Tight little scary circles, back and forth. One direction, then another. The amount of pain it's causing him is obvious from his cries and squawks, but he doesn't stop. If anything, he speeds up.

Hamish is suddenly terrified. 'Why's he doing this, Jess?'

'I don't know,' I admit, my stomach clenching. 'I don't know!'

Walking. Walking. Walking. Twigs won't stop. A few minutes later he's still on the move, but so weary that he can barely hold his head up any more. Brushing my knee with his neck, he utters a faint *mwwwaaa*.

Angus can hardly watch. 'Why won't he stop?'

'Oh, Jess, is he doing all of this for you?' Lucy asks me. 'To prove to you he's all right, even if he isn't?'

My body runs all hot and cold with fear at the thought of that, and I pick Twigs up and hold him close. 'Twigs, you're not doing that, are you?'

Twigs, totally worn out, relaxes against me with a *pffftt*, and softly kisses the back of my hand.

'It's OK,' I murmur, my tears flowing freely over his wings. 'It's OK, Twigs. I want you just to rest. Please just do that. Please.'

The twins and Lucy make room for me as I place him back on the mattress. From there Twigs lets out a single terribly quiet sigh as his head sinks into my pillow. Then his blue eyes crinkle and close as he falls into a deeper sleep than ever.

The doorbell rings around midday. Dad answers it.

'Is it OK if I see how Jess and Twigs are doing?' It's a warm voice: Mrs Baldwin's. I should have known Dad would let her know what's happening.

'Of course it is,' he says, and we hear their slow tramp up the stairs.

As soon as she peeks inside my room, and sees us all sitting around, Mrs Baldwin says, 'Oh, I should have realised you'd all be here. I'll leave you in peace with Twigs. I'm intruding . . .'

'No, no,' I tell her. 'Do you want to sit down?'

Mrs Baldwin hesitates a moment before nodding. 'I'll only stay a little while,' she promises as the twins make room on one of the chairs. She winces at the sight of the sleeping Twigs, but before she even has a chance to ask questions the doorbell rings again and Dad goes back down to answer it.

'I'm sorry I'm so late,' comes a voice, and despite everything we all smile.

Danny.

He's made it to us at last.

He's still apologising to Dad when he enters the room. Then he stops. 'Oh . . . I . . . I didn't think

197

Twigs would be like . . .' He drops his head. 'I couldn't come any sooner, because my uncle—'

'It's OK,' I tell him. 'Please. Just sit with us.'

There's a scuffling noise outside the bedroom door. 'Sorry,' Danny mumbles as Kim pokes her wet nose around the entrance. 'I'll take her out if you think she'll bother Twigs.'

'No, she can stay too,' I tell him. 'Just hold her lead to be on the safe side.'

We soon realise there's no need to hold Kim back from Twigs, though. She trots up in her usual way at first, but stops short when she sees him. Sniffs, then backs off. She looks at Danny for reassurance. When she sees none in his eyes she sits on her haunches, whines a couple of times, and tucks her tail between her legs.

'She knows,' Danny whispers. 'She can tell how bad it is. Dogs always know.'

Soon after that Dad gets a phone call from Alfie Parks. I can hear from Dad's side of the conversation that it's not the first time he's asked after Twigs. Dad brings us sandwiches and drinks after the call ends, squeezing himself and the plates into the one remaining patch on my bedroom floor.

I take my hand away from Twigs' face a moment, and look around the room. All the people who know Twigs well are together in the same place. Which feels good. *Feels right.*

A few minutes later, as if to reward us, Twigs finally stirs.

Opening his eyes, he sits up.

We're so excited that we all surround him, and can't stop talking – quietly, though. We don't want to scare him.

'Hey, Twigs.'

'You're awake.'

'How do you feel?'

'You're looking better.'

'Way, way better!'

We're all speaking at once, our affection bouncing off the walls.

The truth is that Twigs is not looking better, but no one wants to think or talk about that. We're just glad to see his eyes open. We all chat to him at once. I don't even know what we're saying. Little whispery reassurances, that's all.

'I think Twigs is enjoying being the centre of attention, as usual,' Mrs Baldwin remarks, but she can see as well as the rest of us that Twigs is too sick to even know he's getting any attention.

His wakefulness only lasts two minutes before he slumps on his side again, and this time when he falls back asleep he's so still that it's hard to tell if he's alive or dead.

The atmosphere in the room turns icy with fear.

An hour passes and Mrs Baldwin has to pick up her

daughter from the train station, so she heads off. She lightly brushes her fingers across Twigs' crest as she leaves.

'Will you stay?' I ask the others, and of course they do.

It's around two o'clock in the afternoon that Twigs finally wakes again. Dad is in the living room when it happens, but runs upstairs when he hears us calling him.

He arrives just as Twigs is shuffling upright on his claws.

Twigs' left wing drags lower than his right, but he hauls it off the bedclothes and stands there for a moment. Just stands there on the bed.

Then he stares at me.

'Something's wrong,' I whisper.

'What does he want to do?' Hamish asks. 'Walk around again?'

'No. This is . . . different.'

Twigs doesn't seem restless this time. He's just looking at me. He's looking at me as if this might be his last chance to do so, and suddenly I'm terrified.

Then he turns around, and stares at everyone in turn.

Why's he doing that? Why is he looking at each of us so solemnly? I wonder.

I let out a little scream, and Twigs answers it.

He mutters, 'JESS.' Even now he's trying to reassure me.

He bumbles across the bed towards my lowered hands. Rests his head against them. Gazes mildly into my eyes. I can usually tell what Twigs is thinking, but right now I have no idea, and it's so frightening.

He totters to the edge of the bed. When he gets there he glances over his shoulder at me.

'What does he want?' Danny murmurs. 'To go down on the floor again?'

But Twigs isn't staring down at the floor. He sniffs. Something has his attention, and suddenly all our eyes shoot to what's lying against a cushion on the bed.

'The papaya!' Angus cries.

Twigs hops across to where the fruit is piled. He takes a small, tentative bite of the papaya. Then he spots a frond of leafy alfalfa peeking out from under a pillow. He digs at it cautiously with his beak.

Everyone's standing up. I can't stop my heart from hammering.

Kim runs up to Twigs on her big floppy paws. She gazes hungrily at the papaya. She licks her lips. Wags her tail at Twigs.

'Ffffffffff.' Twigs considers a moment, then daintily offers Kim a slice of papaya from his beak.

She takes it from him, tries it, hates the taste, spits it out.

Twigs shrugs, burying his beak deep in the rest of the ripe papaya. After a while he smells some flower blossom juice brought over by Lucy. The juice is in a plastic container. Twigs waits patiently while she opens it and places the juice in front of him.

His tongue darts out, *slurp-slurp*.

He carries on sipping and slurping, then stops, gazing at us all again.

'Pftttt,' he murmurs.

No one speaks. Grunting, 'Nutter,' Twigs hobbles across the bed to grab a brazil nut. He digs it out of the crack of a cushion with his right claw.

I daren't say anything. Not one thing.

'Is he going to be OK?' Angus whispers.

Danny bites his lip. 'Jess? Is he?'

Twigs hops clean off the bed. He winces as he lands on the floor – the bump obviously hurts – but that doesn't stop him waddling like a duck across the room. He finds what he's looking for.

The new rattle the twins brought.

He picks it up in his left claw and bashes it against my knee. Then he gives it a shake. A gentle shake is all he can manage, but it *is* a shake.

'SHUT UP!' he tells the rattle, waggling it around. 'SHUT UP!'

'Is he going to be OK?' Lucy can hardly speak.

'COOCHY-COOCHY,' Twigs sings at the rattle.

'Yes,' I say.

'COOCHY!'

'I think . . .'

'COOCHY!'

'He . . .'

'COOCHY-COOOOOOOOOOOOOOOO!'

'Is!'

Eighteen

It takes months for Twigs to completely recover from his injuries.

Mr Stevens shows me how to replace the dressings and bandages around his chest, but Twigs keeps pecking irritably at them. He's a bad patient. He hates being cooped up. We keep finding him sneaking off to his climbing frame for a quick run about.

But he *does* recover, and the bandages finally come off one bright Sunday morning.

Danny and Lucy help remove them. First the tiny plasters on Twigs' feet. Then the thick bandage almost swallowing his chest.

Once that's gone, and Twigs can freely spread his

wings again, there's no waiting – he simply opens up his beautiful long wings and takes off.

'Roo. Roooo. Rooooooo . . .'

The first flight is short: only a silent little glide taking him through the open door of the living room into the kitchen.

'Twigs! Careful!' I shout as he lands.

After that there's no stopping him, though. He flies between the bedrooms. He flies past Danny's head. He flies down the stairs. He skims past a poem Lucy is writing, plucks it right out of her hand, and in mid-flight drops it again at her feet.

He doesn't care what he bashes into. Walls and doors – so what? He just gets up again, spraying dust everywhere.

'RAAAAAAAAA!' He bangs into banisters. He flaps around the bathroom light like a mad moth.

Just after lunch he knocks Dad down as he's leaving his bedroom.

'Great,' Dad laughs ruefully, hauling himself off the carpet. 'Dive-bombing's back. No one's going to stand a chance now he can fly!'

Not that Dad minds too much. Things have improved between him and Twigs. I've even caught him playing with Twigs once or twice in the evenings – little games that have changed the way Twigs responds to Dad. He's much gentler in Dad's company. Either he's partially melted Dad or Dad's melted him,

I'm not sure which it is, but it's lovely to see.

It's the middle of the afternoon – with the sun still shining – when Twigs shocks us by getting outside. The living room window is only just ajar, but Twigs nudges it wide enough to slip through.

'Uh-oh,' Lucy says, and we all rush into the garden.

I manage to grab Twigs and bring him back inside, while Dad drives to a DIY store and buys plastic sheeting. We tie that between trees and walls. It's tricky getting it just right, but eventually we cover up a large part of the garden so that Twigs can be outside without the risk of him flying off.

It's a warm day, and Twigs flutters around in hesitant circles at first, returning all the time to nuzzle me. He's after reassurance, but it doesn't take many words of encouragement before he's off again, exploring the roses.

He inspects a thorny bush. He spots a shiny green clothes peg he's had his eye on from the bedroom window for weeks.

'*Herrroooo darling!*' he says, just the way Gran used to when she was greeting anyone she hadn't seen for a while.

A light rain shower starts up, falling against the outside of the plastic sheeting. It brings Twigs fluttering back inside the house, but even the rain doesn't bother him much. As soon as the shower ends he's out again, licking droplets of water out of the daisy-heads.

'He looks so . . . happy,' Lucy says, clapping her hands together.

Danny grins. 'Freedom! That's what it is!'

A couple of crows and sparrows are hanging around the garden. They ogle Twigs through the clear plastic sheeting. Twigs toddles along a branch to get closer, and stares at them. He looks like a king beside them, some huge and impossible bird of paradise returning in glory to reclaim his kingdom.

When the birds fly off, Twigs flaps back to the lawn and cautiously tastes the lush green grass. Sun dapples the garden trees, and for a whole magical hour he fly-hops as aimlessly as a butterfly among the shrubs.

At one point he lands on a branch. From there he steadies himself, flexes his tail and glances up at the sky through the plastic sheeting. He stares fixedly outward and, whatever he's seeing, it's more than just other gardens: it's beyond all of us, it's somewhere out there in the air behind the houses, something in the sky, something about being a bird.

I realise that one day we're going to have to face the challenge of true freedom and flight for Twigs, but not today.

Finally he swivels his neck and calls sweetly, 'HERROOOOOOOO!'

There's a rustling of feathers deep in the garden trees – a scattering of *paaaas*. Then we realise there's a gap low down in the sheeting, and the sparrows have slipped through to take a peek at Twigs.

They aren't sure about him. Twigs is twenty times their size, after all. He must look like a giant owl after a meal.

'*Paaaaa, paaaa, naaaaaaaa,*' Twigs chirps respectfully, doing a little prance across the lawn before flying across to them. He sticks his face under the leaves, determined to make them say hi back to him.

Most of the sparrows retreat, but two stay.

Twigs, delighted, lifts his wings in greeting. Bobbing his head, he says 'HERROOOO!' When that gets no reaction he tries a softer 'Herroooo!' When there's still no response he squeaks out the titchiest 'Herroooo!' you've ever heard.

One sparrow flits closer. Twigs scrunches up his neck in an effort to keep the volume down, and offers it a mangled tweet. '*Ccccc-wheeet-tttthh.*'

'Twigs doesn't actually think he's a sparrow, does he?' Dad says with a laugh, fixing the sheeting back in place as the sparrows flit away.

'Nah, he's just being friendly,' I tell him. 'We've been hearing the sparrow families out here every day for months.'

Lucy watches Twigs, her hands on her hips. 'He's not scared any more, is he? Not of the outdoors. He's lost his fear of it.'

'Except rain, maybe,' I say. 'I don't think he's ever going to like rain.'

'Maybe not,' Danny whispers. 'But look at him! About everything else he's fearless!'

Danny's right. And one of the things I'm able to do at last is take Twigs with me while I go sketching. Twigs stays in his cage, of course, but he loves gazing at everything. Spring arrives, and I spend weekends in the country fields and lanes on the edge of town, simply drawing whatever interests me. I used to do this at our old home, but now it's better because if I don't have to carry the cage far I can bring Twigs with me.

One Saturday in April I'm the one who finally calls Alfie Parks. Dad hasn't put any pressure on me. It just feels like the time is right to be fair, and not just to Dad and Alfie, but to Twigs as well. He'll be far happier over at Alfie's while I'm at school than cooped up in our house.

'I'm sorry it's taken me so long to ring, Mr Parks,' I apologise over the phone. 'If you haven't changed your mind . . .'

'No, no, I haven't changed my mind at all,' he tells me. 'Come over whenever you like, Jess. Right now would be fine. I'm not doing anything else. I'd love to see the two of you.'

Dad drives us, and we turn up to discover Alfie busily ringing his garden with barbed wire to keep any cats out.

'Thought I'd better,' he says. 'Twigs will be warier now, but it's best not to take any chances, eh?'

I nod, and we play with Twigs for a while together. Then I manage something I never thought I'd ever be able to do – I leave Twigs with someone other than Dad or Gran.

I almost can't make myself do it. I have to slip out when Twigs is distracted. But the interesting thing is that I *can* slip out. Twigs doesn't see Alfie as any kind of threat to me, and is enjoying playing with him so much that he's not watching my every move. There's trust between them.

After the front door clicks shuts behind us I say to Dad, 'Can we stay here?'

'You mean outside the door?'

'Yes. I just need to be sure.'

'Sure of what, Jess?'

I shrug, because I'm not certain what I'm waiting to be sure of myself at first.

Twigs doesn't take long to come looking for me. When I hear Alfie's gentle cockney – 'Hey, Twigs. Hey, hey!' – coaxing him warmly back into the living room from the doorway, it's reassuring because Alfie doesn't know we're outside listening.

But that's not the main thing that reassures me. I already know Alfie's a good man. It's when I hear what happens next that I know everything is going to be OK. When I hear the silence, I mean. Except for a few merry shrieks, Twigs stays quiet. Which tells me everything.

It tells me that Alfie makes Twigs happy.

Over the next week or so Alfie looks after Twigs for an hour or two each evening, and while Twigs gives me a huge squawking-like-mad welcome whenever I return for him he's always incredibly pleased to see Alfie as well. They bond beautifully.

Am I jealous? Of course I am. But I soon realise that Alfie would never take Twigs away from me. He's so good with Twigs, too, that soon I make a big decision: to let Twigs stay for a whole day at his flat while I'm at school.

Followed by a second day, and a third.

And it's fine.

It really is. Not only is Dad able to get his quiet house back but, when I return, Twigs is always totally chilled – which means I can also get out more with my friends.

At the end of the following week I catch myself glancing at the photo of Gran on my bedroom wall. I touch it, and for the first time since Twigs was attacked by the cat I'm able to smile at it again. My lovely

Gran. She'd be crying her eyes out with happiness to see her old Twigsy-Twiglet now. She wouldn't believe how much he's blossomed just by letting other people become part of his life. It's not only that he can fly and go outside, though both those things have made Twigs happy. It's meeting Alfie, Lucy, the twins, Danny and Kim as well. Bringing them into his life has made it so much richer and more varied.

I was wrong: Twigs never just needed me. We've still got each other, but with all these new friends we've both found much, much more.

It's one Sunday in June that we get a special visit. Lucy, Danny, Kim and the twins are all at our house at the time, eagerly awaiting our guest. Angus has been telling us how they've bought a new spider.

'It's a robot Hercules Baboon arachnid,' Hamish explains. 'Runs on batteries. It can sense movement. Walks towards noise, too. We don't even have to be anywhere near it. We're going to set it loose at school next week near Ginty's class.'

'How big is it?' I ask.

Hamish grins. 'As big as a football.'

Lucy rolls her eyes, presses a pen top hard to her bottom lip and puts on what we call her 'poetry face'. There's no point interrupting her when she's like this, and we all just wait for her to raise her head. Eventually, completing a line with a dramatic full stop, she does.

'I bet you can't come up with a poem right now about our new baby hamster,' Angus challenges her.

'Is it really a hamster, or is it a spider?' she asks suspiciously.

'It's really a hamster. Our mate Jaggers gave it to us.'

'What do you want a hamster for anyway?' I ask.

'We've got a powerful new box-launcher for Sid the Snake, but people don't trust us any more so we need a new tactic,' Angus admits. 'We need a real hamster to bring people in close. You know, get their trust.'

Lucy scowls. 'Boy or girl hamster?'

Hamish shrugs. 'Dunno. We've got a naming problem, too. I want to call the hamster Scratcher, but Hamish prefers the name Dreamboat. He reckons that will make the younger kids more likely to stroke it. But that's a stupid name for a hamster, if you ask me. Come up with a poem that includes all of that if you can, Luce.'

'Easy,' Lucy says. She's much more confident since Professor Alexander Holme of King's College, London invited her to send verses to his students' poetry circle. Apparently she's already mailed a whole series called *Forgotten Shoes, Broken Combs and Leftover Wrapping Paper*.

While Lucy is scribbling away, Danny yawns and Kim, sick of waiting for the dog biscuits to be doled

213

out one at a time, steals the rest of the packet he's been holding and runs off with it.

Danny sighs, absently flicking Twigs' tail.

'Scratcher or Dreamboat,' he mutters. 'Tricky choice of name. I'd pick the name Maurice for a hamster if it was me. What do you think, Kim?'

Kim is still sucking up the dog biscuits, but she wags her tail at the suggestion of the name Maurice. To be honest, though, Kim always agrees with everything Danny says.

Twigs decides he's hungry, and it's while I'm sketching him in a tug-of-war with Kim over the final dog biscuit that our visitor arrives.

Not a human visitor.

A bird.

And not just any bird.

A hyacinth macaw. Blue and majestic, with a fine crest almost as large as Twigs'.

Mandy Walnut.

Her arrival has been planned as a big surprise for Twigs for weeks.

We told Alfie all about her, and it didn't take long before he paid Bertrams a visit. She's with Alfie for weekends, but this is the first time she and Twigs have met.

With a twinkle in his eye, Alfie releases Mandy straight onto the living room carpet.

'She's roughly the same age as Twigs,' he tells us. 'A

beautiful mimic, too. Picks things up incredibly fast. She only said hello when I first got her, but I've taught her a few more phrases.' He grins as we all gather around. 'And, unlike some birds I can think of, she's very well behaved.'

'VERY WELL BEHAVED!' Mandy repeats loudly. 'VERY WELL BEHAVED.'

Her neck stretches high as she looks us over.

But it doesn't stretch half so high as Twigs'! As soon as he sees Mandy his head *boings* up and he lets out an ear-crushing, 'GALA-GALA-GEENY!'

I think he's going to hop-wobble towards her, but no. Instead he does a stylish little glide, cleverly using only a few tail feathers.

Mandy bobs her head, as if to say, *Very impressive*. At least, from her wobbly dance around him, I'm pretty sure she thinks that. They keep this up for a few minutes, racing in opposite circles.

'YOU'RE GORGEOUS!' Twigs finally screams.

'YOU'RE GORGEOUS!' Mandy screams straight back.

'VERY WELL BEHAVED!' Twigs yells.

'YOU'RE GORGEOUS!'

When Mandy keeps saying that, Twigs starts running up and down the room incredibly fast – and Mandy follows him.

'WHOA!' Twigs squawks.

'WHOA!' Mandy repeats. Struggling to keep up

with him, she yells, 'NICE CUPPA TEA! LOVELY JUBBLY! OH YES! NICE CUPPA WILL DO FINE!'

Twigs is mesmerised by this. His beak opens and closes in total admiration.

'NICE CUPPA TEA!' he croons.

'LOVELY JUBBLY!' she tells him.

'YEAH!'

'NICE!'

'YEAH!'

'CUPPA TEA!'

'VERY WELL BEHAVED!'

'NUTTER!'

'NUTTER!

'NUTTER! NUTTER! NUTTER! NUTTER! NUTTER! NUTTER!'

And they're off. What is it with talking birds and the word *nutter*?

Once she starts, Mandy won't stop saying it, and neither will Twigs. It's crazy in the room for about a minute, then there're a few more dashes around the carpet from the pair of them.

That's followed by what I can only describe as a crafty expression. It comes over Twigs all of a sudden. At the same time he stands tall on his claws, turns his head almost upside down and gazes between his legs right into Mandy's eyes.

'Swishy-swoo,' he murmurs in a velvety voice.

216

'*Mwwaaa,*' she almost purrs back.

Twigs waves his wings delicately at her, then comes out with this: 'MOO-MOO- YAYAYAYAYA!'

'YAYAYAYAYA,' she whispers.

'He's chatting her up,' Angus says, open-mouthed.

'No way!' Hamish cries out.

'I swear he is.'

Alfie laughs. 'He's a smooth operator, that one.'

Dad arches his eyebrows. 'Romance? It'll never happen, will it? Surely they're both too old.'

'Mm, it'll be interesting to see what develops between them,' Alfie remarks dryly. 'I can bring Mandy here occasionally, Jess. As long as Twigs behaves himself, that is.'

I glance at Dad.

'Once a week. For two hours only,' he tells me firmly. 'I mean it. Not one minute more. I can tell they're both going to be insanely noisy.'

Twigs twists his head upright again and gazes dreamily at Mandy. 'SHUT UP!' he shrieks at her.

Mandy opens her beak. 'VERY WELL BEHAVED!'

'WHOA!'

'YOU'RE GORGEOUS!'

'NUTTER!'

'YOU'RE GORGEOUS!'

'NUTTER! NUTTER! RAAAAAAAAAAA AAAAAAAAA!'

Twigs suddenly gets so excited that he leaps onto a chair, bites it, raises his head and lets out an unbelievably happy *squonk*.

'GIVE UZ A KISS!' he screams at Mandy and, surprising us all, she does.

Epilogue

NEW-BORN

Little tail, little feet,
Little heart, little beat.
Here he (or she) is,
Just been born,
Baby hamster, in the morn.
Dreamboat by day,
Scratcher by night,
The name Maurice Dreamboat Scratcher
Doesn't sound quite right.

Lucy Daniels

the
orion star

Sign up for **the orion star**
newsletter to get inside information
about your favourite children's authors
as well as exclusive competitions and
early reading copy giveaways.

www.orionbooks.co.uk/newsletters

Follow on

Orion
Children's Books